# Broken Sky

## Part Eight

**Chris Wooding**

Cover and illustrations by Steve Kyte

SCHOLASTIC

**Other books by Chris Wooding:**

*Crashing*

*Point Horror Unleashed: Catchman*

*Kerosene*

*Endgame*

£5.83

J129,137

Scholastic Children's Books,
Commonwealth House, 1-19 New Oxford Street,
London WC1A 1NU, UK
a division of Scholastic Ltd
London ~ New York ~ Toronto ~ Sydney ~ Auckland
Mexico City ~ New Delhi ~ Hong Kong

First published in the UK by Scholastic Ltd, 2000

Text copyright © Chris Wooding, 2000
Illustrations copyright © Steve Kyte, 2000

ISBN 0 439 01494 8

Typeset by M Rules
Printed by The Bath Press, Bath.

10 9 8 7 6 5 4 3 2 1

Check out the

# Broken Sky

website

**www.homestead.com/gar_jenna**

# Broken Sky

SA'ARIN

JEDDA

UR-LAN

# 1

## Divided in Many Ways

The seething red orb of the sun had sunk to a thin, burning arc over the horizon, but in the desert the temperature was still hot and the air was dry as powdered bone. Distant rock outcrops broke the uniformity of the land. The shadows of the dunes loomed long across the smooth sand, and lizards skittered to their holes for the night, leaving S-shaped trails behind them.

The oasis was a wide, uneven swatch of trees and bushes that thrived in the lee of a low, weathered wall of red rock. Whatever ancient upheaval that had thrown up the jagged barrier had also opened a route to an underground stream, and since then the rock had protected its companion, guarding it against the slowly marching drifts of sand. Sheltered, a lake was formed in the hard, dry earth; and with it came plants, tough-barked palms and hardy bushes that bore spiky-skinned fruit.

Jedda stood on a rise in the land, just past the edge of the treeline, looking out over to the desert. Behind him, torches flickered in the shade of the oasis, illuminating windbreaks and canopies that stretched between the stout trees like spiders' webs. Laughter and chatter drifted through the dusk. To either side of him, some way off, disruptor posts stood guard.

A rustle behind him alerted him to a newcomer.

"Greetings, Kia," he said, and turned around to meet her.

She could almost have been a different person to the dirty, unkempt creature they had rescued three days ago. Her hair had been shorn after she was sold to the Overseer of Osa'ara Mines – the name, she had learned, of the place she had been imprisoned – in case of fleas or lice. In the year since, it had grown back in filthy, matted locks. Jedda's people had managed to clean and style it into an elegant, feathery cut that flattered the lines of her face. The green of her irises had been picked out by a soft, subtle eyeshadow, and she wore a silk desert-gown of iridescent black.

"You look beautiful," he said.

She laughed uneasily. "I don't suit these things at all," she replied. "I am grateful, but Li'ain has offered to give me some of her more practical clothes when I see her next."

"It seems a shame," Jedda replied. "I think they suit you perfectly. And as you were apparently reluctant to use a mirror, you left me no choice but to offer you the services of my maids in making you a little more presentable. They are not used to such . . . independent spirits as you and Li'ain."

"I'm honoured," she said, walking up to stand next to him, looking out over the endless sea of sand. "But I'm a mountain girl at heart, Rai'kel Jedda."

"Ah," he replied. "So you know."

"What, you were thinking of keeping it a secret?" She looked at him in vague disbelief.

"No. I merely wanted the opportunity to make

an impression on you before formality got in the way."

"Formality? Because you're a Rai'kel? I hadn't noticed. Li'ain never treats you like . . . what is it, royalty?"

"Not royalty," he replied. "Kings and Queens are royalty. The Rai'kel are more like shepherds. Each nomad tribe has one. We are the generals, the leaders, the arbitrators; but more, ours is the final say in where the tribe moves next. We are nomads, Kia; our destination is the most important thing in our lives." He paused, his dark eyes narrow as he scanned the horizon. "But no, you are right, Li'ain does not afford me the respect that my people do. That is what I like about you north-folk."

"That we don't have any manners?"

"Exactly," he said, with a smile.

Kia laughed again, genuinely this time. "I'm glad that's settled, then. So what are you looking for? Sa'arin?"

"Sidewinders."

"Sidewinders?" she repeated.

"We are not so far from the front line of

Macaan's forces that we can afford to relax. The Sidewinders are the vehicles he uses to scout the deserts for our camps."

"Don't you have sentries to do that kind of stuff?" Kia asked.

He turned to look at her for a moment, amusement on his face. She felt slightly uneasy beneath his gaze. "I like this time of the day," he replied. "Looking for Sidewinders is just my excuse. The desert is beautiful at dusk."

There was silence for a time, as they stood together, watching the sun inch its way out of sight.

"You came here to ask me something," Jedda said.

"I'd like to know a few things," she admitted. "Both you and Li'ain haven't exactly been straight with me. I appreciate all you've done, but I also realize that you did it for a reason. I'd like to know what that reason is."

"Takami," Jedda replied. Kia had expected to have to argue, or at least to prise the information out of him that she wanted. His immediate response put her a little off-balance; it was a few moments before the name he had spoken sank in.

"What about him?" she asked, her voice frosting.

"He leads the assault against the desert-people. He is Macaan's commander in the south."

Kia was silent. Her previous good humour had gone; her demeanour had become cold and hard.

"I will explain," he said. "Macaan has been a threat to the desert-folk ever since he first conquered the Dominions. But the deserts are vast, and we as a people move around all the time. He had no stronghold to assault, no weak points to exploit. It would take an immense amount of manpower to subdue every tribe in the deserts, because we are so spread out. But, like the Noman tribes of the steppes, our dealings with the central continent have always been cordial. Our ways of life are too different; the city folk have little interest in us, and we owe no allegiance to them."

"So you did nothing, while Macaan took over," Kia said. A faint voice of caution warned her against accusing a Rai'kel in his own land, but she ignored it.

"It was hardly as simple as that," he replied in a level tone, turning his face towards hers. She met him with her own angry gaze, and was ashamed to feel herself softening as he looked at her sympathetically. His unhurried words, his calm eyes, his dark features, all spoke of a quiet and reassuring power that made it difficult to mistrust him. Kia felt irrationally guilty for the implication she had made.

"So how was it?" she asked, sounding like a spoiled child to her own ears and not knowing why.

"The greatest strengths of the desert-folk are also their greatest weaknesses. We are divided in many ways, and not just by geography. Macaan could not hunt us all down, that is true; but neither could we organize to defeat him. There were too many vendettas, too much bad blood between the tribes. We had been separated far too long."

"Why do you talk about it like it's in the past?" Kia asked, looking back out over the horizon so she did not need to look at him, so she could conserve some of her precious anger.

"Macaan is invading *us* now. That is a powerful spur for unity. Not the central continent, a land we cared little about; he is in our territory. If there is one thing you will learn about the desert-folk, it is that there are few things dearer to us than territory. Have you not thought why the Overseer of Osa'ara Mines allowed even convicted criminals a room of their own? No other mine would waste the expense. And why none of the Taskmasters were allowed inside? Not even a dungeon grants such privileges."

"You have different rules of privacy," Kia said, catching on. She had begun to notice this during her few days with the tribe, though she had been kept mostly separated from other people. "You have only fabric for walls, so there is more respect for others' personal space."

"It may seem like idiocy to you," the Rai'kel said, "but if the Overseer had not made those rules, he would have trebled the chances of a riot or a revolt. A person's tent, their patch of land, their possessions – it is taboo to violate these things without permission."

Kia stirred the sand at her feet with the toe of

her sleek black sandal. "And you're saying that the tribes would gather together against Macaan, now that he is invading your territory."

"Oh, he has been here for a long time, Kia. Six seasons now, eighteen months. The advancement is slow, far slower than when he took the cities to the north; but he has made many conquests, and sent many to Osa'ara Mines. There is only one remaining problem."

"The Sa'arin," Kia guessed.

"Ah, the Sa'arin," he said, half as a sigh. "Yes, they have been a plague to the desert-folk ever since we can remember. One of the dangers of living as we do."

"What are they?"

"Nobody knows. Desert spirits, it is said. There are certain places, we have found to our cost, where they will not permit us to travel. Before Macaan came, they were content to keep to these areas. If we tried to cross them or settle there, the Sa'arin would rise up and drive us out. But now . . . since Macaan's forces began their invasion, they began to attack our camps. At first, we were defenceless; then the Machinist's Guild told us of a new invention they had come up with – the disruptor posts. They were willing to provide the tribes with enough to protect themselves . . . for a price, of course. Furs, silks, rare things they could trade." He shifted his weight and turned back to look over the darkened oasis, listening to the laughter and merriment within. "I cannot speak for the other tribes, but in our own case it was only just in time. Maybe they sensed what we were going to do and hoped to stop us before we got our defences up. I do not know. The Sa'arin launched a great offensive on us. Many died before all the disruptor posts were activated. It was only then that the Sa'arin were driven back." He lowered his eyes. "My people are resilient. Listen to them; only a day has passed since the Sa'arin killed twenty of their brethren, and they can still celebrate and make merry in this place. I will not allow myself to fail them. My only concern is their happiness and survival."

Kia watched him for a moment, finding herself studying his face with interest. A sudden clutch of guilt grabbed at her, and Ty's face replaced Jedda's in her mind.

*What was she thinking?*

"They were after me," she said, needing to speak to distract herself. Her voice came out harsher than she had intended. "Takami, my brother, is leading the invasion force; the Sa'arin attack your camp just after I arrive and I can *hear* them *talk*. This is *no* coincidence, Jedda, so if you're any kind of Rai'kel then you tell me what I've got to do with all of this. *Now*." She found herself flushed and angry again; he seemed to have an effect on her that robbed her of her usual self-control, and made her swing wildly across the spectrum of moods in a way that was unfamiliar to her. The feeling was disconcerting; she didn't like having no say over her own emotional state.

"You have a right to be angry at me," he said. "I agreed to help Li'ain free you for my own selfish ends. I wanted your help, and I wanted Parakka's help. I did not think of the person I was dealing with, only of the welfare of my tribe. I apologize."

"Then tell me what you want," Kia said softly, feeling inexplicably humbled by his words.

"I want you to stop the Sa'arin killing my people," he said. "And I want you to help us free our land. I want you to help defeat Takami."

Li'ain sat cross-legged at the edge of the lake, enclosed in her own private booth by walls of coloured fabric that hung between the trunks of the surrounding palms. A gap had been left as an entrance; the other side was open to allow her a view across the water, to the dark shore not too far away, where torches cast their flames among the ripples. A fire burned in the scrub, and next to it was an open canvas knapsack with food and drink inside. She waited, thinking, with a wooden cup of summerleaf wine in her hand. She had been expecting company for some time, and now the tread of footsteps on the ground beyond the fabric walls told her it was here at last.

"I thought you would find me sooner or later," she said, by way of an invitation to the person outside.

Kia stepped in purposefully, still dressed in her desert-gown. "Good, then we can dispense with the pleasantries and get down to business."

"Sit, if you will," Li'ain offered, motioning with one hand towards the empty space by the fire.

Kia obliged, arranging her gown with some difficulty around her legs.

"You don't seem at all at ease with that," Li'ain observed good-humouredly. She herself was attired in baggy trousers of a dark, heavy cotton and a simple, sleeveless black top, accentuating her tall, slight frame.

Kia gave her a look over the crackling fire. "Listen, Li'ain. You've been good to me, and I appreciate that. Cetra knows what would have happened to me if I had stayed in that place. But I'll only be pushed so far before you have to level with me. I know you've got some plan. I want the whole story, now, or whatever cooperation you *think* you're gonna get ends here."

Li'ain smiled, brushing her long, black hair back over one shoulder. "You seem to have recovered your old fire remarkably quickly," she said.

"You never knew the old me. Don't sidetrack."

"I told you before, Kia, I knew you by reputation. That is why I got you out of the mines."

"Let's start there, then," said Kia, relentless. She wasn't giving up until she had all the answers this time. Allowing others to take the reins of her life, back in Tusami City after her father's death, was what had got her into the nightmare of Parakka's war in the first place.

Li'ain reached over to her knapsack and poured a cup of wine, offering it to Kia. "It is not poisoned," she said, seeing Kia's momentary reluctance. Kia felt a little foolish for considering it, and she took the cup.

"No more delays. Tell me."

Li'ain put down her own cup of wine and stood up, turning around so her back was to the fire. She reached over her shoulders and gathered up her black top, pulling it upward to reveal the smooth curve of her spine. Pale green stones caught the light, studding the gaps between her vertebrae. Kia counted five visible, but she could not see above the base of Li'ain's shoulder-blades or below the belt of her trousers. She guessed by the arrangement that there were three more; spirit-stones were always set symmetrically, starting from the exact mid-point of the back.

Li'ain pulled her top down again, arranged herself in a cross-legged position again and continued, the fire flickering between them, making shadows lunge and stab at their faces, tingling their skin with its warmth as the temperature around them began to fall with the loss of the sunlight.

"I am a Fetch. My stones allow me the ability to 'visit' other locations for a brief few seconds. I usually use that time to take something. As you can imagine, it makes me quite an exceptional thief."

"I've never heard of that."

"There is much you have not heard of, Kia."

"You were the one who was putting those things in my room?"

She nodded slightly. "Things that were precious to you. I had to make you remember . . . enough to want to make your way out. I visited you as you slept, from time to time. Your dream-talk was very revealing."

Kia let pass the unease she felt at the thought of having a stranger watch her as she slept.

"You gave me the keys to get out?"

"How else would I know to be waiting for you?" Li'ain countered simply. When Kia did not reply, she continued. "I work for neither Parakka nor Macaan," she said, her words tinged with the strange, cut-glass accent that she carried. "Everyone has a story to tell, about how the King's forces did this or that to them: destroyed their farm, killed their brother, sent their son to the mines. Their reason for wanting the end of Macaan. Yours is common knowledge, Kia. Mine . . . does not matter. All I know is that the children of Banto have been a rallying point for Parakka and the people ever since the Integration. Stories are still told about your fighting at the Ley Warren and in defence of Base Usido, Ryushi has become known as the one who slayed Aurin, and—"

"He *what*?" Kia exclaimed. "He got her?"

Li'ain briefly explained how Fane Aracq, the Princess's palace in Kirin Taq and the seat of her power, had been overrun by Parakka and the Keriags, and how Ryushi had torn the stone from around Aurin's neck before plunging his sword deep into her black heart and throwing her body from the spires.

Kia laughed involuntarily as she finished. "You believe that?" she asked incredulously.

"I am aware that some . . . elaboration might have occurred," Li'ain admitted.

"Well, as much as I may be out of touch with my dear twin, I can tell you that he *didn't* 'throw her body from the spires'," she replied, still chuckling. "He's hardly so melodramatic." Her mirth faded a little. "There were rumours that he was in love with her," she said, almost wistfully. She snapped out of her reverie and focused again. "Heh. I'm talking about him as if he were still around. He thinks I'm dead. I don't know where he is; I've only got your word that he's still alive. He could be a different person if I ever see him again."

Li'ain had turned away from the fire to look across the lake, and her face was black with shadow. "He is still alive," she said. "Though I do not know where he is right now."

"Take me to him," Kia hissed, suddenly urgent, grabbing Li'ain's wrist around the fire. Li'ain took a sharp breath and turned back to her, surprised; and she saw in Kia's eyes a sudden, animal desperation.

"I will," she said, breathing it like a promise. "But there are things you must do first."

"What things?" Kia asked, releasing her slowly and sitting back.

"Takami's invasion of the desert is only a decoy," Li'ain said. "His forces are far less than the desert-folk believe. Takami is an inexperienced commander; indeed, he has failed Macaan before now. The King is up to something else . . . I do not know what, but it has to do with the Machinist's Citadel." She looked into the fire, and the rising heat lifted wispy hairs around her face like frail, stirring wings. "Losing his daughter has made him insane. I believe he intends to do something terrible. Only you can help these people, Kia. Only with your powers can they beat Takami. You talked peace to the Keriags, Kia. Talk peace with the Sa'arin."

"What makes you think I can?" Kia asked.

"There is only one type of stone that the desert-folk possess," Li'ain said. "Their beliefs do not allow them to introduce foreign matter into their bodies. It is taboo. But those that ride the *mukhili*, the giant desert-beetles, they wear Bonding-stones, similar to our wyvern-Riders. Their stones are set at the base of their skull, beneath the hairline. Jedda has one."

"I know what mukhili are," Kia said. There had been several in the service of Parakka, mobile fortresses that had proved invaluable both at the Ley Warren and Base Usido. "Go on."

"But outsiders have come to the desert many times. Some of those outsiders have had stones like yours . . . stones that can manipulate the earth. Three times now, it has been said that these people have heard the talk of the Sa'arin; to two of them it was as indistinguishable mutterings, but one could even understand it. He, however, did not have the craft to reply. He had three stones. You have six."

Kia did not reply.

"Do you not see, Kia? The Sa'arin are entities that take their shape from the sand. They speak *through* the sand somehow. Only those who are attuned to the earth can hear them. The others had not half your power, Kia. You may be able to speak to them, make them see—"

"Why?" Kia interrupted bluntly.

"Why?" Li'ain repeated, uncomprehending.

"Why bother? What's your angle? You aren't from the desert. Why do you owe these people?"

"I owe," she said. "That is all you need to know. Except that Takami holds all the passes out of the desert to the north, and nothing gets through there. You could run from this, Kia, if you wanted. Nobody is forcing you to fight for us. But nobody would help you cross the desert, and nobody would help you get through the passes."

"Who said I wanted to run?" Kia said. "I was going to help the moment you told me Takami was here. But not for you, or for Jedda. For Ty." She closed her eyes, her brow creasing in determination. "Takami killed him. I have to even the score."

"I think we all do," Li'ain said, and the fire snapped loudly.

# 2

## The Fusion of Metal and Flesh

It was a vast natural cavern that they walked into, beaded with rows of glowstones that clambered over the contours of the roof like a net. The air was cool and damp, and rang with the sharp, fizzing echoes of cannon-rams as they battered at the rock wall. Ryushi, Quain and the others were travelling along a wide central thoroughfare, following a series of rails designed for mine-carts. The rails ran along a thick spine of stone that crossed the cavern like a bridge. To their left and right, there was a long drop to the ground. Beneath them and to either side, a chaotic network of roadways, tiers and ledges had been constructed, a haphazard mess made with no thought for design. And wherever the eye roamed, there were ur-Lan.

21

They were strange creatures. Distinctly humanoid in appearance, but there was something about them that made Ryushi unable to think of them as sentient, feeling beings. Perhaps it was the mechanical way they moved from task to task, or the way that they never talked to each other or even acknowledged each other's presence. Their features seemed normal, but they were oddly lifeless; they did not grimace with the effort of lifting a rock, or flinch if a piece of stone chip from the wall hit them.

They were squat but grotesquely muscular, about five feet high and probably four feet across the shoulders. Their skin was a sour yellow-white, and they were completely hairless. Each of them wore a narrow, low-light visor, a strip of black glass inside a frame of metal. And most of them carried cannon-rams, heavy cylinder-drills that fired short pulses of energy into the rock to break it up. The rain of sparks whenever they were used formed a shifting pattern of light to counteract the steady glow of the stones overhead.

"Can they see us?" Ryushi asked, as Quain brazenly walked down the thoroughfare towards the other side of the cavern. Several ur-Lan were approaching them from the other direction, pushing mine-carts loaded with rubble.

"Oh, they can see us," Quain said. "Won't do nothin' about it, though. Not big on smarts; just do what they're made to do."

"Made?" Calica queried, keeping her eyes on the ur-Lan that were nearing them.

"We grow them in the central vats," Quain said. "Tailor-made to requirements. They're clones, is what they are."

And now the approaching ur-Lan were near enough to see that, yes, their features were indeed identical. The intruders stepped aside to let the mine-carts pass. The ur-Lan did not give them so much as a glance, heading past them towards the tunnel they had come from to dump their cargo.

"I'd heard of clones as a theory," Gerdi said. "Didn't think anyone would be sick enough to *try* it."

"Why do you think you heard about it at all?" Quain replied. "We've been usin' clones for years in the Citadel. They mine out raw materials for us. We've got Breed, as well. Vat babies, you might call 'em. Artificially inseminated embryos, grown in controlled conditions. Much brighter than the ur-Lan. Property of the Citadel. We use *them* for the technical stuff." He smiled nastily, then tapped a few studs on the metal half of his face. "I'm just gettin' static down here. When we get up out o' the mines, I'll get a signal."

Gerdi looked around at the ambling, half-alive creatures in their ceaseless industry. "Don't you guys have *any* ethics?" he asked.

"Who needs ethics?" Quain replied. "We've got science."

As promised, the mines were occupied almost exclusively by the ur-Lan, and Quain and the others went on their way with very little trouble. Only once did they have to dodge out of the way of a pair of Guardsmen, who unexpectedly appeared on a rock ledge above them. Quain grumbled that Macaan's men had no business being here, but Calica counted them lucky that two inattentive Guardsmen were the worst they had to deal with. They reached the main cargo elevator without any further incident, a vast, flat metal platform surrounded by a chest-high set of railings and a gate. Quain halted them there, tried his communicator again, and shook his head with a phlegmy murmur.

"We'll have to go up. There'll be guards at the top, no doubt. Better take the service stairs; coming up on that thing'll alert just about the whole Citadel."

"I can handle the guards," Gerdi said.

"Well, let's hope you can," Quain said, leading them towards a thick metal door that was set deep in the rock near by. Another row of dials faced him, only four this time. He set them and hit the palm-stud, and the door hissed open.

"Still know a thing or two," he muttered to himself, and went inside.

The service stairs were cold and dark, a simple set of metal steps that right-angled their way upward around a square shaft. The occasional striplight cast a damp sheen across the rock. Gerdi wrapped his own glowstone and replaced it in his pack. Quain tried his communicator again halfway up, but to no avail. He tutted and murmured something about too much stone blocking the signal.

There was another door at the top. Gerdi held out a hand.

"Wait here," he said. "I'll go check."

With that, he hit the palm-stud – no code was needed from the inside – and stepped through, closing the door behind him.

They listened in silence for a moment.

"You think the boy'll be alright?" Quain said.

"He'll be alright," Hochi replied bluntly, and again Calica had almost forgotten the hulking man was there with them. She resolved to have a talk with him after they got back to Gar Jenna. This broody silence was not like him at all.

They heard voices on the other side of the door. There was a Guardsman there, just as Quain had predicted. They could hear Gerdi talking to somebody; but to the person he was talking to, he would sound completely different from the fourteen-winter Noman boy that they knew. Gerdi's talent was for illusion; he could appear and sound like anything he wished, provided he had seen it first. But his stones could only alter the perception of those he was concentrating on. The person on the other side of the door was probably seeing and hearing him as a Guardsman right now, but to Quain and the others he still sounded like – and would still look like – Gerdi.

After a few spoken exchanges, they heard a few raps on the door. Calica palmed the stud, and there was Gerdi, beaming at them.

"I am *so* the best," he announced modestly.

"What did you say to him?" Ryushi asked, looking up and down the wide corridor that they had emerged into. Close by was a pair of huge bay doors marked with a brass plaque bearing the legend: "Cargo Elevator".

"He did it all for me," Gerdi said. "Asked if I was the relief shift. I said yes, so we talked a bit and he left. Surprising how easy it is to fool some people."

"I'm happy for you, Gerdi, but why don't we get out of here before the *real* relief shift turns up?" Calica said.

"Hey, you're a pretty smart chick when you try," Gerdi grinned. It was a comment calculated to annoy, but Calica was strangely heartened by it. At least he still had some of his old animation left in him. Perhaps his subdued manner was just because he was worried about Hochi.

Quain had assured them that the lower levels of the Citadel would be sparsely policed, if at all. He was right. After a time, they stopped jumping at every clank and hum in the dark, gloomy metal corridors and began to relax a little. They made their way upwards through layers of apparently deserted storerooms and laboratories, Gerdi scouting ahead. There were plenty of side doors and shadowy tributaries to make evading the occasional wandering guard or Machinist an easy matter. Macaan had still allowed the folk of the Citadel to go about their daily business – the whole place would have ground to a halt otherwise – and the denizens of the Citadel were not exclusively Machinists. If they were seen, especially in the company of Quain, it would be assumed that they were a group of traders or businessfolk who had been engaged in the process of bartering for Machinist technology when Macaan invaded, and had not been allowed out. The Machinists were, after all, a purely mercenary organization.

Still, it was a risk that it was better not to take.

"I'm gettin' a signal!" Quain declared suddenly,

and hurried them into the nearest unlocked doorway. It led to a room stuffed with unidentifiable bits of rusted machinery, lit by a single white striplight. They crowded round him while he tapped the tiny studs across his cheek, and spoke in a quiet mutter, loud enough for their benefit.

"Any Machinist within range, respond," he said. He knew he would get several replies by making such a general call, but the transmitter device would filter the codes of every attempt and allow only the highest-ranking Guild member through.

"Quain," came the thin, reedy reply. "It has been a long time since you dared to enter the walls of the Citadel."

"Who is this?" he demanded. "You're not transmittin' any code."

All Machinists except those of the highest ranks automatically put out an identifying code when transmitting; it was how the other voice had known who Quain was. But *this* stranger put out no code at all. Perhaps he had struck lucky.

"What is your business here?" came the reply.

"I said, who is this?" Quain reiterated.

"Someone who knows that you left to join Parakka many seasons ago, and that you are a traitor to the King."

"Well, I plan on stayin' that way, so if you don't have anything else to say then get off my channel."

"You're here to find out Macaan's plans?"

"Why won't you transmit your code?"

"In case anyone is listening who should not be. It would be best if Macaan did not know I was here."

Quain paused and harrumphed, casting a quick glance around the others. Ryushi's look said: *Should we be worried?* Quain waved him off with a dismissive gesture.

"I know what Macaan intends to do," the voice spoke again.

"Let's hear it, then."

"Not while others might be listening. I have an associate; you must meet him."

Quain barked a laugh. "I don't reckon so. I've seen less obvious traps in my time."

"Then don't talk to me. Talk to him. You may remember him, in fact. I'm transmitting his code now."

Quain adopted a listening attitude for a few moments, the human side of his face frozen attentively, and then the connection was cut. He briefly explained the conversation to the others, who had been unable to hear the voice at the other end.

"You know whose code it is?" Calica asked.

The old Machinist frowned. "He was still a youngling when I left, but I knew him. Helped me out sometimes in the tubestreamer labs. A Breed by the name of Chiro."

"You think it *is* a trap?" Gerdi queried.

"Breed take orders from the highest-ranking Machinist, and follow them to the death if they have to. I may've left a long while ago, but officially I still kept my rank. See, we don't owe any loyalty to Macaan. We jus' want the money to finance our work. No one cares if one of our members join Parakka; they're jus' "on leave". They're still part of the Guild." He coughed. "If that mystery voice isn't a Machinist, Chiro'll take orders from me over him. If it *is* a Machinist with a higher rank than me . . . no reason not to trust him. Nobody in the Guild is goin' to want to help Macaan."

"Still sounds suspect," Gerdi mused. "I guess we got no choice."

"As ever," Ryushi commented. Choice was a luxury he had come to miss.

"Call him, then," said Calica. "You have a place we can meet? Somewhere you both know? You'll have to tell him without actually saying it over the transmitter."

"I know where, don't fret," the old Machinist replied. "Let's jus' hope it's only him that turns up."

Ryushi was shocked by how much of the Machinists' immense stronghold was actually derelict or in disuse. The Guild seemed to simply discard rooms when their usefulness was completed and build new ones over them. They had ascended many levels since the mines, and yet there was still a vast amount of wasted space, including whole laboratories that looked like their occupants had simply dropped everything and left several years ago.

It was in one such room that they waited now. An enormous, cylindrical device that looked like a cannon of some kind loomed over everything, surrounded by workstations and heaps of notes and charts. The cannon was sealed at both ends, with numerous riveted hatches and glass sections that were so grimy as to be almost opaque.

"The tubestreamer," Quain said, patting the flank of the huge device as if it were a favourite pet. "Worked on this for two years, on 'n' off." He looked it over, sighing to himself. "S'posed to be able to analyse spirit-stones, determine their mineral content. Find out the different compositions of different stones. The first step to makin' 'em ourselves."

"I don't think the Deliverers would have been too happy about that," Calica said.

"Well, they had nothin' to worry about. Never worked. Then some breakthrough had the Master Machinist off in another direction, and we decided what we were doin' wasn't worth hangin' on to. So we dropped what we were about and went to work on the disruptor posts instead."

Ryushi looked around the gloomy laboratory, his arms folded. "Weren't we supposed to meet someone here?" he asked.

He was answered by a clank as a grating was pulled loose somewhere in the dark recesses of the laboratory. Automatically, he and Calica drew their swords.

"Seems he's already here," said Quain.

Chiro emerged from the shadows at the end of the lab, approaching them warily. Ryushi and Calica looked to Quain for reassurance that this was the one they were waiting for; he waved at them to put their weapons away. They sheathed them with only the slightest hesitation, studying the blank mask of the lean youth's face with naked suspicion.

"Chiro's a Breed," Quain said, in response to their unspoken fears. "If he's been ordered to help us, you can trust him more 'n you can trust *me*."

Ryushi felt faintly abashed. He had met Kirins, and suffered none of the prejudice that Hochi had. He had talked with Iriqi, a Koth Taraan, and treated it no differently to a human even though it was far, far from being one. Yet the fusion of metal and flesh that the Machinists inflicted upon themselves and their kind still made his blood run cold, and he could not help feeling uneasy talking to one. Even Quain, who could scarcely be more down-to-earth, had his moments.

"I have instructions to tell you what I know about King Macaan's intent for this facility," Chiro said, his voice shredded by his mask.

"Good to see you again, Chiro," said Quain, cracking a smile and slapping him on the shoulder. "You've grown, alright."

"That has a tendency to happen, over time," Chiro replied neutrally. "It is good to see you, too, Section Keeper Quain." The words were a politeness; he didn't really feel any way about it.

"Well," said Quain, looking around at those assembled. "We've come this far to hear what you've got to say. No sense in wastin' any more time."

"When Macaan first invaded the Citadel, his choice of tactics made it seem obvious that he had a single objective before all others," Chiro began immediately. "To capture and hold the Pulse Hammer. Subsequent actions have put this assumption beyond all reasonable doubt."

"The Pulse Hammer?" said Quain. "That was

only a pipe-dream when we were working on the disruptor posts."

"It was the technological advances made during the development of the disruptor posts that led to the Pulse Hammer."

"The Guild actually *built* it?" Quain exclaimed, and gave a low whistle of awe.

"And we're talking about *what,* exactly?" Gerdi said, making a prompting notion by rolling his hand in a circle.

"The Pulse Hammer," Chiro replied obliquely, and ignored him in favour of Quain.

"What d'you reckon Macaan wants with that thing?" the Machinist mused.

Chiro turned the flat planes of his face slowly away from him. "Only two scenarios seem likely. Either he plans to cross the sea to other lands, or exercise his secondary option."

Silence for a moment.

"Run that by me again?" said Gerdi, butting in. "*Cross* the *sea?*"

"The Pulse Hammer is an experimental prototype. It is intended as a defence mechanism for the Dominions against the possibility of an attack by Deepwater creatures, but it is also the model for many smaller versions, which will be installed on ships around the Dominions. When activated, it sends out a pulse through conducting rods that run through this Citadel, far into the earth. From there, it will travel out from the continent into the sea, into Deepwater."

Hochi breathed an oath at the mention of the name. Chiro continued in his expressionless monotone, as if he were reading the explanation from a script without any enthusiasm.

"In Deepwater live creatures of sizes far beyond those encountered on the mainland. For a long time, the only information about them came from myths of the Marginals – the coastal folk of the Kirin Taq – and the sailors of the Dominions."

"That's because any ship that goes out there gets swallowed whole!" Gerdi interrupted, incredulous. He turned on Quain. "What are you guys doing messing about in Deepwater?"

"Hear him out, Gerdi," said Calica.

Chiro waited for Gerdi to calm and then continued. "Theoretically, the Pulse Hammer sends out a frequency so low that only underwater creatures of a certain mass will we able to hear it; its bandwidth is too broad for the tiny aural sensors of most known marine life. The effect will depend on the volume and speed of the pulses. It has been supposed that by bombarding a certain area of the sea with pulses, the Deepwater creatures will be forced either to dive to great depths or to vacate the area temporarily. To their ears, the sound of the Pulse Hammer has been likened to that of a human standing next to a magma derrick."

Ryushi had seen the magma derricks in Tusami City; immense towers of iron with massive metal hammers inside that pistoned ceaselessly up and down. Chiro's analogy was a good one; he knew that he would not be able to stand being next to one for long without being driven deaf or insane.

"The Machinists have created something to keep the Deepwater monsters at bay?" Calica asked, amazed. Both the Dominions and Kirin Taq had always been isolated continents, with any exploration further than six miles or so offshore being impossible. Sailors would not sail out of sight of land anymore. Every ship that had gone that way had either never come back or been badly crippled by the immense beasts that lived out there. The Deepwater monsters seemed to attack anything that trespassed across their territory. But if what Chiro said was true, then . . . then the Pulse Hammer could be the catalyst for a whole new age of exploration, the key to the geographical barrier that had kept the Dominions – and its counterpart, Kirin Taq – locked in. A small model could be installed on a ship to repel the creatures away from it, allowing safe passage.

"But why build a big one first?" Calica asked.

"As insurance," Chiro replied. "There is no telling how the Deepwater creatures will react if we begin sending out ships equipped with these mechanisms. This giant prototype is intended to keep them from our shores if they should decide to attack us."

"That's the theory," said Quain. "Works on the Sa'arin; could well work on the Deepwater monsters. But there's somethin' else, right, Chiro?"

"You said he could either cross the sea or. . ." Gerdi said.

Chiro nodded. "If the pulse is kept at a low power, it will not be strong enough to cause the Deepwater creatures the amount of discomfort necessary to drive them away. In fact, it will merely enrage them; as of someone playing constant, discordant music in the adjacent room to the one in which you sleep. It can be supposed that they will seek the source of the noise and destroy it."

"Mauni's Eyes!" said Gerdi, stealing Hochi's favourite exclamation. "The Deepwater monsters will come *on land*?"

"And they'll be plenty angry, too," said Quain, and cleared his throat. He looked at the shocked faces around him. "Meaning there's not goin' to be much left of the Dominions when they're done."

"But they can't come on land! They live in the sea!" Gerdi protested.

"Sailors have reported Deepwater monsters with legs several times," Chiro replied flatly. "And this being the case, it has been speculated that there are air-breathers among their numbers. If Macaan should decide to try and draw in the Deepwater monsters, he will set the Pulse Hammer up to pulse to the east. The creatures will come in across the steppes, and across the central continent, laying waste to everything in their path. There is no telling what kind of destruction it will cause. It is surmised that only the deserts will be safe."

"But why? Why would he do that?" Ryushi asked.

"Irrelevant," said Chiro. "He cannot activate the Pulse Hammer according to his plan."

"Why not?" asked Calica.

"Because I," Chiro replied, "have the one thing he needs to make it work."

There was nothing at first.

Then the sensations began creeping back. Warm and wet. Like a womb. Thick-skinned bubbles barged past him, running up his body and then jumping free to soar upwards. His eyes crackled and came on-line, and that was when he *knew* he was dead or dreaming. He was floating in a soupy ochre ooze. There was movement beyond the ooze, but it was filmy and distorted.

For a time, he could not remember his name, who he was, what he was doing here. Where *was* here, anyway? He put out a hand, the movement feeble and frail. His fingers touched glass. So that was what was keeping the ooze around him. The glass was a large window in a metal tank. That alarmed him for some reason.

A face appeared in front of him, a figure, distorted by the curvature of the window. He tried to guess who it was, but his disorientation still clung to him. The figure pressed a stud on the outside of the tank, put his hands behind his back, and leaned forward so that his pale, white-haired countenance became clearer.

"Okre Jey," said the melodious, sinister voice through the crackle of the intercom. "You really should learn to kill yourself more efficiently."

The Master Machinist howled and bucked inside the tank, the confusion in his head tattering and falling away, but the movement exhausted him within seconds and he hung limply in the ooze.

Macaan regarded the small figure with a scornful expression. The withered body was suspended in the yellow-green culture fluid of the vats, attached to a multitude of tubes and cables that sprouted from every part of his body, sewing in and out of his mottled veins. The trunklike cable that ran from where his mouth should have been to the respirator pack on his chest had been supplemented by several others. Two thin, clear tubes ran into the two metal intakes on his inner elbow, where he had received food intravenously after his mask had been installed. They throbbed with a white fluid.

*"How?"* came the broken, mechanical croak over the intercom.

Macaan sighed, as if having to explain things to such an incompetant was terribly tiring. "Your self-destruct system was as out-of-date as the rest of your parts," he said. "You only managed to burn out a few components. Some of your workers were persuaded to give you an overhaul. They even fixed your eyes. It's amazing how much your Augmentation process is like the Conversion that my Jachyra have to go through.

43

The only difference, really, is that they get the full-body treatment. Oh, and they don't have a choice."

"*Conversion is simply the name for introducing a certain set of Augmentations into a Resonant,*" the Master Machinist said wearily. "*Your Jachyra all have the same Augmentations. Most Machinists would consider the work done on them . . . excessive.*"

"I like to think of it as the wonders of technology. After all, if you were not mostly machine, we could not have brought you back, now could we? Your own vats took care of the needs of your biological parts."

"*Why have you done this, Macaan?*" The faceless form of Okre Jey floated before him like a pathetic ghost.

"You left before we could finish our business," Macaan said. "Don't worry; even your vats cannot sustain you for more than a few days. The replacements on your parts were hasty and temporary. You *will* die. But not until you call that Breed Chiro and order him to bring the cortex key to me."

*"I will never do that."*

Macaan turned away from the tank, motioning to someone out of Okre Jey's range of vision. "Obviously, I did not expect you to concede so easily. That is why we installed a few special components when we were rebuilding you. Pain amplifiers, for one. Would you like to see?"

The seven-foot figure of Vore stepped into view, his back disconcertingly straight, as if a rod had been shoved down his spine. He was holding a crude brass handset with a dial and several buttons on it.

*"I will never help you against the Guild!"* Okre Jey wheezed hoarsely.

"I did hope you were going to say that," said Macaan. Vore twisted the dial and Okre Jey screamed as the torture began.

# 3

## The Skeleton Stays

"What are we *doing* here?" Ryushi muttered, stalking around in the gloom.

"Waiting. What does it look like?" Calica snapped, feeling faintly irritable herself. Her nerves were frayed. Bad enough that they had to hide in a half-lit laboratory, sitting amid all the discarded junk of another failed Machinist attempt at changing the world, while Gerdi, Quain and Chiro went to go and pick up the cortex key and find the source of the alarm that wailed incessantly through the Citadel. Bad enough that she had to keep on glancing over at the dark, silent hulk of Hochi, who was sitting like a statue in the shadows, his grim presence making her uneasy. She could do without Ryushi complaining as well.

The wind-siren had started up out of nowhere, making them all jump. It was supposed to be easy; once Chiro had told them about the cortex key, it would have been a simple task to take it out of the Citadel, beyond Macaan's reach. That would have ended the threat of the Pulse Hammer, at least for long enough so they could deal with it. Chiro had hidden it somewhere, he told them. It was too risky to carry it around.

"If it's that risky," Ryushi had said, "why don't you just break it and be done?"

"My orders stated that it was preferable to keep the cortex key intact. I will only break it if there is no other choice," Chiro had replied blandly.

"You know how valuable a cortex key is? Probably costs as much as a large town," Quain had put in.

"You're weighing *that* against the chance that the whole of the Dominions might be destroyed?" Ryushi had cried.

"No sense in throwing money away unnecessarily," Quain had replied.

Calica was unable to understand the attitude of the Machinists. They had no regard for ethics or morals, nor any standard of what was right. Nobody dared stand up to them, because they and they alone provided the cogs and gears that made the world run. The Guild saw that no competition was allowed to exist, and so they had free rein. All they wanted was to create technology, to allow them to make more money and create new and better technology, and on and on in an endless cycle. On the surface, it seemed like they were engaged in the betterment of humankind; but that was not the case. They were simply maniacal toymakers, building for the joy of creation, with no regard for the consequences.

The three of them tensed as another pair of booted feet ran past the door to the tubestreamer laboratory, but the noise quickly faded. Quain had assured them that they would be safe down here; there were so many empty labs and testing-sites that there was virtually no chance of anyone coming in to look for them unless they were part of an organized search. It made Calica feel a little better, but not much. What if they had discovered the entrance that Ryushi had made? Did they know there were intruders in the Citadel?

"What's going on out there?" Ryushi asked nobody. He was just as frustrated as she was. "They've been gone for an hour now."

"It'd take that long just to get across the Citadel," Calica said. "Whatever Quain has in mind had better be—"

She stopped, suddenly scrambling to her feet.

"What?" Ryushi asked. Hochi was also watching her from the shadows.

"They're coming!" she said, her eyes unfocused, looking around the room at attackers that weren't there. "They're coming! Guardsmen! Jachyra! *They know we're here!*"

Half an hour earlier.

Chiro, Quain and Gerdi walked amongst the narrow press of the power coils, great rectangular slabs of tubes and pipes that were arranged like bookshelves in long rows. The space between each coil was a tight squeeze, but they were wide enough to accommodate the three small intruders as they slid their way down the aisles.

"Aren't these things dangerous or something?" Gerdi asked.

"These are only small coils, feedin' power to the local area," Quain said. "The big ones downstairs, now *they're* dangerous."

Their mystery contact had been in touch with them shortly after they left the others in the lab, telling them not to worry about the alarm. Usually, an emergency message would have been broadcast to all Machinists the moment the wind-sirens started up, but that system – like many others – had been down since before Macaan invaded and had not been repaired yet. The reason why the siren had sounded was being spread by word of mouth, and it was taking its time getting around the Citadel.

"It's not you, Quain," said the voice. "The alert has been out for Chiro for several days now, but nobody has yet discovered the presence of intruders. This is a general alarm. News has reached us that the Ley Warrens have been opened. Parakkans and Koth Taraan are swarming through into the Dominions at five key points. Your counter-invasion appears to have begun."

Quain relayed the message to Gerdi, who whooped "Al-*right!*" before remembering where he was. Chiro ignored him, instead changing direction immediately to take them back the way they had come.

"Hey, where are we going now?"

"The secondary objective has been achieved," Chiro said. "We have determined the cause of the alarm. Now we progress towards the primary objective: to retrieve the cortex key."

And so they had ended up in the power coils, taking a scarce-travelled shortcut across a section of the Citadel. The loud drone of the coils and the stifling heat combined with the lack of elbow room made the place uncomfortably claustrophobic, but Gerdi had endured much worse. Only Quain seemed to be flagging a little.

Gerdi looked at Chiro's back and wondered. He was not prone to moments of deep thought, but something about this Breed boy sparked a note of empathy inside him. He'd been told about Breed by a Parakkan Machinist a few seasons ago, but the information had mostly slipped out of his mind. Now he saw Chiro, it all came back to him.

Breed were not clones, like the ur-Lan were. They were the product of the same process that humans were created by; the only difference was, their conception and growth was done in culture tanks instead of bodies. Vat babies, Quain had called them. Did that make them less human than he was? He didn't know. He supposed not, but philosophy had never been Gerdi's strong point. How did you define a human, anyway? For all he knew, Kirins were hatched from eggs; he was fairly sure they weren't, but how did he know? It wasn't like he'd ever actually discussed childbirth with a Kirin. He counted Kirins as human, even if they *did* come from eggs (which they probably don't, he reminded himself before he got carried off in his own theory); so he guessed Breed were too.

But watching Chiro made him think about what the Machinist had told him. About how Breed were brought up to aspire to be machines, how their only purpose was to serve, and serve efficiently and well. They were taught that they had no soul like humans did, that they existed only for the best interests of the Guild. Without the Guild, they would never have been created at all; so the Guild owned them, by rights, and brainwashed them into willing slavery.

It wasn't right. Gerdi could stomach the Augmentations that the Machinists implanted in themselves; he could even see why Machinist children and Breed might *choose* to be Augmented, when non-Augmented folk were practically useless within the walls of the Citadel. But to teach them from birth that they had no soul, that they were not human, that their only value was in serving . . . it made him feel sour inside.

Of course, there was one last thing that the Machinist had told him. Breed were given implants that prevented them from ever leaving the Citadel. If they strayed outside its boundaries, their mechanical parts would shut down and kill them.

*Can't have the slaves running off, can we?* Gerdi thought bitterly.

He frowned as he watched Chiro ahead of him. He had not really been studying the Breed closely, lost as he was in his own thoughts, but now that he did, he saw that there was something peculiar going on. Chiro was muttering to himself quietly, and his head moved from side to side occasionally, making minute nods. As if he were listening to something.

"Come on, we gotta get *out* of here!" Calica cried, looking from Ryushi to the shadowed form of Hochi and back again.

"What about Gerdi?" Ryushi said, as Hochi stirred and got unhurriedly to his feet.

"I don't know about Gerdi. I just . . . I saw us all here, the Guardsmen arriving with Jachyra, we fight but there's too many . . . why are we even *arguing* about this? Have I ever been wrong with a premonition?"

*Not with a premonition, no. But you were wrong one time before; and Ryushi's mother died for your mistake. Kia was the only one who knew about it; she was even going to tell him. But she's dead now. The skeleton stays in the cupboard.*

She felt a momentary touch of the rancid guilt that accompanied the thought, but now was not the time to worry about it.

"I'm not going without him," said Hochi.

"Hochi, if we go now, we can double back

and find him!" Ryushi urged. His hesitation was gone; he knew how accurate Calica's predictions were.

The big man hefted his warhammer on to his shoulder. "I'm not going without him," he repeated.

"Gerdi can handle himself better than any of *us* can in a situation like this," Ryushi said. "Why do you think we let him go with Quain and Chiro? He can disguise himself as anything he wants."

"I'm not—" Hochi began again, but Calica cut him off.

"For Cetra's sake, you idiot! You do what you want, then! I'm not getting myself killed because of your stupid insistence on punishing yourself!" She grabbed the front of his shirt in one fist and pulled his face closer to hers. "You think you deserve to die because you lost a *pendant*? You think Tochaa would have wanted that? Whatever he meant for you to do, if he meant anything at all, it didn't involve *giving up* like this! I've seen more will to live in a—"

She never finished. Hochi backhanded her

across the jaw with a meaty fist, and she was sent crashing into a row of shelves, knocking old equipment about and smashing dusty jars.

For a moment, there was stunned silence. Hochi stood with his arms crossed, a silent man-mountain in the gloom, his eyes buried in darkness.

Then Ryushi reached for his sword. "You *son of a—*"

"*No!*" Calica cried, lunging across to clasp her hands over his as they wrapped around the hilt of his weapon and drew it half from its sheath. "I'm alright, it's okay."

Ryushi did not take his eyes from Hochi, blazing anger glinting in his gaze.

"There's no time," Calica said. "Come on. Leave him, if that's what he wants."

"If we ever meet again, Hochi, we'll settle this," Ryushi swore, his voice thick with rage. Hochi did not move. Ryushi broke away with a snort of disgust, and he and Calica raced out of the door.

Right into the path of the oncoming Guardsmen.

\* \* \*

Twenty minutes earlier.

"The cortex key," Chiro said, pulling the two-foot-long, rectangular sheet of translucent spirit-stone from behind a cluster of pipes. It had a metal handle at one end, like a stunted saw; its surface was etched and grooved with a multitude of interconnecting white lines.

"Good," said Gerdi. "Now can we get out of here?"

"Agreed," said Chiro. They had gone from the close press of the power coils to the even more confining maintenance ducts that ran between the floors of the Citadel. It was in here, a crawlspace surrounded by gently throbbing cables and pipes, that Chiro had stashed the key.

They returned to the hatchway where they had got into the ducts, and rejoined Quain there, who had protested that his joints weren't up to squeezing him through such a confined space. Chiro showed the key to the elderly Machinist, then slid it into the inner pocket of his sleeveless jacket.

"Suggest we head back a different way," Chiro said. "Power coil output may adversely affect cortex key."

"You think it will?" Quain husked doubtfully.

"A precautionary measure," the Breed replied, the mask of his face unreadable.

"I don't care which way we go, can we just hoof it a little?" Gerdi said impatiently. The annoying rise and fall of the wind-siren was beginning to set his teeth on edge.

They set off again through the dim maze of the Citadel's lower levels. The routes that Chiro took them were a little more heavily travelled, but it was still remarkably simple to remain unseen among the side-alleys, serviceways and empty laboratories. The interior of the Citadel was built without any regard for symmetry or design; the corridors were fashioned around the laboratories, and the laboratories were built to whatever specification was needed.

They had not been going for long when Chiro brought them to a halt before a sliding door. "Through here," he said, turning the set of dials on the lock and palming the stud. The door slid open to a darkened room. "The lights are malfunctioning. Keep close to me, Gerdi; I will guide you."

"Gerdi. Chiro. I'm getting a transmission!" Quain said, hurrying in after them, his own vision flicking to low-light as the door slid shut behind them.

"Quain! Listen to me!" It was the unidentified helper. "Macaan got to the Master Machinist. He tortured him into making a transmission! Chiro's orders have *changed*! He's leading you into a *trap*!"

"Appreciate the warning," Quain said, as the lights came on suddenly, blindingly, revealing the twenty or so Guardsmen with their halberds trained on the newcomers, "but I'm thinkin' it just got sprung."

# 4

## She the Accused

{voice}

{!newshe!}

{?newshe?}

{kill newshe}

{hurt we}

{no}

{?no?}

{listen}

She knelt in the sand, just her and the Da'al Jakai. The oasis was perhaps a mile away, but the distance had seemed three times that, trudging over the shifting sand in the blazing heat of the afternoon. Kia had forbidden an escort. She was going, without any guard or protection, into the desert. Jedda and Li'ain begged her to reconsider, told her she was taking an unnecessary risk. She insisted. During the long walk with the silent, faceless Da'al Jakai, she had questioned herself time and time again. Why *was* she taking the chance, exposing herself like this? She could just as easily do this from inside the camp. Out here, the Sa'arin could swamp her.

Part of it was because they knew she had the power to demolish the Sa'arin if they chose to attack. Part of it was because she knew that if you wanted to talk peace with an enemy it was sometimes necessary to do it where the enemy felt safe. And part of her just didn't care anymore.

It could have been Calica, walking out there like that. The choice she had made was what Calica would have done. She had become a warrior like Calica, a politician on the Council like Calica, a diplomat like Calica. She had recruited the Koth Taraan and the Keriags to the side of Parakka, and now she was going to try with the Sa'arin.

*I've become the person I hated*, she thought. *The person who killed my mother.*

Or had she just been unconsciously imitating the one that she had suspected her twin to be in love with, even from the start? Was it all rooted in jealousy, like Ryushi had said when they last saw each other? She had Ty, but she would not let another girl have her brother. And it had driven them apart, in the end.

*And if what Gerdi and Elani said was true, Ryushi had fallen for Aurin. Calica's Splitling. So it was all for nothing, anyway.*

All for nothing. Just like everything was. All the effort, all the struggle, and what was the point? She was tired. She just wanted an end to the heartache.

And so she knelt like a statue, with a Da'al Jakai standing before her, his hands on her head like a benediction, the multicoloured rags of his robe stirring around him, his blank mask painted in colours of fire. It was dusk, and the raging orb of the sun was touching the horizon, painting the dunes in sultry heat and long shadow. She slept the trancelike sleep, and the two figures were motionless, alone, a tiny speck in the ocean of sand.

In a circle around them, eight Sa'arin rose silently from the ground, one for each point of the compass.

Dream and reality were indistinguishable. The Da'al Jakai had created a landscape inside her head that was exactly as it would be if her eyes were open. But only in her subconscious could she hear the Sa'arin clearly, and only when she was in the trance could she talk to them.

Over the last week, while she had been trying to establish a way to communicate with the creatures, she had found that her dreams were plagued by the conversations of the sand ghouls; but while awake, she heard them only rarely, and then she had no way to talk back. It was her dreaming that attracted them in the first place; they recognized the threat of her as she unconsciously vocalized incoherent sounds in the sand, trying to answer questions that were not directed at her. The language of the Sa'arin was in the shifting and vibration of the sand; their voices were the scratch of the particles moving across

each other. It worked on some level that she
could not understand, and try as she might, with
all the distractions of awareness, she could not
see a way to reply in a way that they would
understand.

But while she slept, her unconscious mind was
doing what her conscious could not. It was
adapting, working ways to use her power to make
real words, as a baby learns to use its mouth for
more than squalling. This morning, she had
woken, remembering the conversation she had
had the night before, when she had *said*
something to them . . . and they had replied.

*{I can hear you}*

*{!newshe!}*　　　　*{!newshe speaks!}*
　　　*{!newshe!}*

　　　　　　　　　　　　*{newshe!}*
　　*{My name is Kia!}*

And then her eyes had snapped open, and it was

gone. That day, a Da'al Jakai had arrived from their monastery across the desert and asked to see her. He had been travelling for three days.

She didn't pretend to understand. She couldn't make sense of it. Another facet of the Da'al Jakai? It didn't matter, anyway. She was sick of trying to fathom the mysteries of the world. Resonants, Deliverers, Da'al Jakai, Jachyra, Koth Taraan, Keriags . . . in the two short years since the destruction of Osaka Stud, she had been exposed to more wonders and strangeness than she had ever dreamed possible, and she knew she would never have the answers to half of the questions that she had about them. She and Ryushi had been so unbelievably ignorant when they had started on this journey, but the war that they had been thrown into had opened their eyes. Sometimes, all she wanted to be able to do was shut them again.

But she couldn't. In her dream, as in real life, the eight Sa'arin surrounded her, as if they were a council of judges and she the accused. Except that in the dream, the Da'al Jakai was nowhere to be seen.

To speak, with a mouth that she did not have. It wasn't so hard, not in the environment of calm and peace that the Da'al Jakai provided for her. She had already done it several times for a golem, stringing grains of earth together to form a rudimentary larynx. The Sa'arin spoke in the ancient desert-tongue, which made matters easier. Perhaps, in whatever age they had gained the ability to communicate between themselves, they adopted the humans' language rather than inventing their own. It was only natural; every culture was made up of elements cannibalized from others. But it meant they were a young race, younger than humankind by a long way.

Kia steeled herself. The Sa'arin were silent. *All* of them. No distant whispers, no muttering, no nothing. A whole race waited.

Time to begin.

It was dawn when she returned to the oasis. The black was bleeding out of the sky, paling to blue and lightening rapidly, and the trunks of the palms were still dark with the shade of their neighbours' leaves. A warm wind slid across the desert, bringing scatters of sand rolling up the slopes of the dunes and blasting off their crests in loose, powdery clouds. The glowering sun was just raising itself over the horizon, shimmering with distant heat-haze. And out of that sun came Kia and the Da'al Jakai, two dark, tired figures shambling towards sanctuary.

A lookout spotted them and, on the Rai'kel's orders, sent a man to wake Jedda and Li'ain; but others came as word spread, and by the time Kia and her companion had reached the edge of the treeline, a sizable reception awaited them. Jedda greeted Kia with a gentle embrace, treating her delicately as he saw how exhausted she was.

"You need to sleep," he said. "Your tent is ready."

"No," she said. "No, let's get this over with. There's no time."

"What do you mean, there's no time?" Li'ain asked.

"I mean Takami's coming," she said. "His forces are moving south."

They took her to a clearing by the lake, which had been used in recent days as a conference area for Jedda and his aides. The Da'al Jakai stood near by; he had nothing to say that Kia would not say. The clearing was little more than a wide swathe of thick, water-fat grass, broken up by the occasional low bush or shrub. Fabric walls had been set up among the trees, but these did little to block sound. Strange how the desert-folk valued privacy so much yet found secrecy almost impossible because of the way they lived.

Kia sat down on the grass, her short, feathered hair in disarray, and looked over the lake as Jedda, Li'ain and several others sat down in front of her, with many more standing nearby and watching. The rising sun was sending white, burning glints off the surface of the water. A flock of brilliant blue wading-birds were plumbing the shallows for fish. A six-legged lizard, the size of a large dog, lapped at the water's edge, while several skittish desert cats wound in and out of the trees at the shore, sizing up the lake as if it were something dangerous, to be approached with caution.

*This place is beautiful*, Kia thought. *Why can't I just stay here? Why all the cursed struggle?*

She turned back to the assembly. "I'm not going to mince words," she said, raising her voice. "We don't have the luxury of wasting time on the niceties of diplomacy. You are an honest people; I will be equally honest with you." She paused. "Macaan and the Machinists have conspired to trick you. The disruptor posts are not the defence against the Sa'arin that they are supposed to be. They are the *cause* of the Sa'arin attacks."

There was a general murmur, but no outrage. They were a remarkably well-controlled group.

"How can that be?" Jedda asked. "The Sa'arin were attacking us *before* we used the disruptor posts."

"No," said Kia, turning her deep green gaze on the Rai'kel. "They were defending themselves."

"Please explain."

"Your people call the Sa'arin desert spirits. It's true, to an extent. They are not physical beings but *forces*, rather like one of these." She put out a hand casually, and a small golem, only a few feet high, rose out of the ground towards her palm. Once formed, it walked off towards the lake and

69

into it, disappearing in a slowly spreading pool of mud. "That golem had no mind of its own; it was controlled by one brain – mine. But somewhere, somehow, out in the desert, these things have been evolving. The Sa'arin are the brains that control the creatures you fight."

"But what *are* the Sa'arin?" Li'ain asked.

"They're too small to see," Kia said. "Microscopic crystalline organisms that live in the sand. By rights, they should be mindless specks; but somewhere along the way they gained the ability to link up with one another. Each Sa'arin is made up of billions of these specks. They become vast circuits, networks of incredible complexity; in essence, just like the human brain. Different organisms become synapses, nodes, neural pathways . . . and sooner or later, they develop an intelligence. They pass on information by resonance, each particle vibrating at a certain frequency; and they can affect the sand and earth just like my spirit-stones can."

There was silence. She swept her gaze over the assembly, and rested it on Jedda.

"But as you have discovered through the disruptor posts, they can be disrupted by bigger vibrations. That is why they attacked you when you travelled to certain areas of the desert. They cluster in areas where the mineral content in the sand is right for growth. You were treading on them, and they feared that. Because with men come machines, and with machines come vibrations, and that means death for them."

She rolled her head wearily around her tired shoulders, waiting for somebody to say something. Nobody did. Only the wind stirred.

"They talked in dreams to me. I think the Da'al Jakai translated most of it to pictures in my head. I don't know. Most of what I know is what they told me, but they knew only their side of it. I filled in the blanks myself. But let me tell you what *they* saw. They knew humans were intelligent like themselves, but they had no way of communicating with us. So they were content to fight us off their land, and hope we would take the hint and stay away." She shifted on the grass. "Then the machines came from the north. Macaan's advance invasion force. The things they feared had arrived at last, and not only that. They brought with them the disruptor posts."

"Which only made them angry," said Li'ain.

Kia nodded. "Exactly. Not only are the disruptor posts a constant, unending annoyance to the Sa'arin, they are a reminder of what will happen if the humans begin planting them over their territory. Several dozen Sa'arin clusters have been unwittingly destroyed already by Takami's forces. The Sa'arin do not have sides, or allegiances. They could not differentiate between the desert-folk and Takami's men. They were all human, so they were all enemies."

"And then the Machinists' Guild offered us disruptor posts to defend ourselves, and that made it far worse," said Jedda. He was calm, but there was an anger bubbling underneath the surface. "Why?"

"Money," said Kia. "At least, that's my best guess. Macaan struck a deal with them; he would use disruptor posts to stir up the Sa'arin, and the Machinists would then make the profit selling them to you as a means of defence. It would be a mutually beneficial arrangement. The Machinists would get their money, and Macaan would have made the Sa'arin mad enough to kill."

"But surely the Sa'arin would attack Macaan's men too?" Li'ain said.

"Macaan's men have force-halberds. You only have swords. The Sa'arin are not much of threat to a well-armed force." Kia shrugged. "He just wanted to keep you busy, while he conquered the Dominions. All he had to do was give you enough problems of your own so that you wouldn't bother him in the central continent. Why do you think he never invaded far south? He was just holding the passes. He knows he can't get all the nomad tribes on their own territory; he just wanted you out of the way."

"So why attack now?" Jedda asked.

"As to that," Kia said. "Your guess is as good as mine. But the Sa'arin tell me that the force to the north is on the move, and we are not so far from the frontline."

Jedda tapped his lips thoughtfully with one finger. The assembly around them was mesmerized, unsure whether to even believe the casual revelations that Kia was offering them. But it was as she said; she was not in the mood to make what she said palatable. They could accept or not. It was their choice. They waited to see what their Rai'kel would do.

"You have told us what the Sa'arin have thought, and what they are," he said at length. "But what will they *do*?"

"I explained to them the difference between Takami's men and yours; how you do not use heavy vehicles or equipment, how you respect the desert. They will give you safe passage to battle Takami. It is a temporary truce. After that, depending on what occurs, they will talk further. But the first thing they will demand is the deactivation of the disruptor posts."

"They know I cannot do that. They are testing our integrity," said Jedda.

"Takami is the problem," said Kia. "Drive him away. I have only laid the first stone to the bridge between you and the Sa'arin. But no more will be laid until he is gone."

Jedda frowned, thoughtful again.

"We have only the Sa'arin's word that they will not attack," he said. "It may not be enough to convince the other Rai'kel to band together."

"You said it yourself; the Rai'kel have forgotten

their quarrels in the face of a greater enemy," Kia said. "You still have the disruptor posts active – your camps will still be protected."

"It is the posts that *attract* them."

"No, it's the posts that torment them. That is why they attack – to rid themselves of the pain. But they are still an effective defence."

Jedda paused thoughtfully, running his fingers over his cheek. "I need guarantees."

"You'll have me," said Kia. "And the Sa'arin know I can wipe them out."

Li'ain looked from Kia to Jedda.

"You have to try, Jedda," she said softly.

Jedda nodded. "We must move. Takami might be here within days. I will pass the message on to the other tribes."

"How?" Kia asked. "You can't possibly reach them all."

Jedda motioned at the Da'al Jakai. "They have their ways," he said, and the faceless mask dipped once in acknowledgement, before the multicoloured figure turned and disappeared into the trees.

"Now we wait," said Jedda. "And we prepare."

# 5

## Into the Firing Line

The bolt of force hammered up the corridor like a land-train, stripping the surface of the walls as it tore into the ranks of the Guardsmen, blasting them aside or pulverizing them where they stood.

"Hochi! They're *here*!" Calica shouted back through the open doorway, drawing her sword. One side of her jaw was darkening to an ugly violet.

"Let's *go*!" Ryushi said, grabbing her arm and pulling her after him. "There'll be more of them coming!"

"But he's—" she began to protest.

"*Leave* him," said Ryushi, through gritted teeth. "He's made his choice."

Calica cast a last glance back at the doorway, and then ran with him. Ryushi shook his head in disbelief. Hochi *hit* her; he'd actually *hit* Calica. Over the past few months (or the last couple of hundred cycles, he corrected himself; he fell so easily out of the habit of counting in Kirin time) he had become less and less attached to Hochi. He supposed it had started a long time before that, when Hochi had first begun to obsess about Tochaa's parting gift to him; the pendant which held the symbol of Broken Sky. But recently, even Gerdi had become frankly scared of him. Now *this*.

Whatever their friendship had been before, it crumbled the moment he hit Calica. He'd made his bed. Let him lie in it.

He released Calica and drew his own sword as they fled down the corridors, running from drab, grimy light to faint shadow and back again as they passed the striplights on the ceiling. The heavy footsteps of armoured Guardsmen sounded from behind them now; already those who had escaped Ryushi's blast would have clambered over their shattered comrades and swarmed into the tubestreamer lab.

"Ryushi! Eyes front!" Calica cried, as four

Guardsmen stepped out from a side corridor and into their path. They had obviously not expected to find their targets running towards them. The moment of surprise and hesitation cost them. Two fell as Calica and Ryushi's blades blurred in tandem, deep gashes carved into their chestplates. Calica pulled her sword free in one smooth stroke, bringing it up and into the chin of the third Guardsman, smashing through his helmet. Ryushi's sword was buried too deep, lodged in his victim's armour, and a quick tug could not pull it loose. Instead, he lunged weaponless at the last Guardsman, but his target had already dropped his halberd. Ryushi slammed him up against the wall, his hand over the Guardsman's heart, the force energy gathered just beneath the skin of his palm.

"Please. . ." the Guardsman said, and it was the voice of a young man, probably only eighteen winters like Ryushi himself. "Please . . . I didn't want to be this . . . I didn't want to be a Guardsman. . ."

Ryushi's face softened a little, and Calica felt a warm squeeze of sorrow blanket her insides. How many Guardsmen like this had they killed, Dominion folk who had simply been taken from their parents by Macaan, because they were unfortunate enough to be male and have the blue spirit-stones of force given to them? Was this all part of the Deliverers' idea of balance? That they would give blue stones at the *pah'nu'kah*, knowing that Macaan would most likely take the babies for his armies?

Ryushi withdrew his hand from the Guardsman's chestplate. "Get outta here," he said, and the Guardsman ran back into the side-alley he had come from. Ryushi pulled his sword from the dead man's chest by bracing his foot against the corpse, and looked hurriedly over his shoulder, where the sounds of pursuit were almost upon them.

"Any ideas?" Ryushi asked.

"The corridor," Calica said. "Wreck it."

"Out*stand*ing," Ryushi said with a grin, and he reached out with his hand splayed wide in the direction they had just come, and suddenly bunched his fingers into a fist. The metal on all sides punched inwards, as if a giant claw was crushing the corridor in an immense grip, and with a deafening screech it crumpled. Girders and junk from the floor above clattered in after it, blocking the corridor behind them completely.

They fled back through the Citadel, never quite sure where they were going, only that they were heading down. The alarm was wailing all around them, and they were certain that if it had not been sounding for them before, then it certainly was now. Every so often, Calica would recognize a place where they had been earlier, and know which route to take. It was not so much from memory – the sprawling, random corridors of the Citadel all looked the same – but from her postcognitive powers. She sensed that they had passed that way, and divined the direction they should head next.

Without Calica's navigation, they would never have had a hope of finding their way out. As it was, it was still little more than dumb luck that brought them to the cargo elevator. There had been no new skirmishes on the way; once they had lost themselves in the lower levels of the

Citadel, it would have taken more men than Macaan had to find them.

But someone had guessed where they were going, alright. Nothing else could explain the force that waited for them at the elevator to the mines.

Ryushi swore explosively as he ran round the corner into the wide corridor that led to the cargo elevator. The huge bay doors at the end were standing open, and arrayed there were perhaps twenty Jachyra and forty Guardsmen. The Guardsmen opened up on him the minute he came into sight; Calica grabbed his arm and yanked him back into cover a moment before the force-bolts smashed into the metal wall of the corridor in a salvo of dull impacts.

Ryushi rubbed the long, sap-stiffened locks of his hair anxiously. "They're not fooling around out there," he said, a little breathless from his near-escape. "Thanks."

"No problem."

He dared a quick peek around the corner, and then quickly drew back into cover. The door to the service stairs that they had used to come up was on the other side of the wide corridor, across the firing line. "They're not moving."

"They've got us pinned," said Calica. "Reinforcements on the way, no doubt. You think you can take all of them?"

"Probably not," he admitted, then a grin spread across his face. "But I do have a plan."

"Oh good, I like plans."

"You remember the combination for the door to the service stairs?"

"No," she said. "Quain opened it. I'm fairly sure I can get it, though."

He peeked out again. "That'll have to do. See, most of the guys out there are actually standing *on* the platform of the cargo elevator. I'm gonna see if I can trip the switch. Nobody's guarding the service stairs that I can see."

"You want to race the cargo elevator down to the mine floor?"

Ryushi shrugged. "Sure. It can't be that fast."

Calica smiled, then winced as the bruise on the side of her face twinged. "Go for it," she said. Ryushi actually seemed to be *enjoying* all of this; his anger at Hochi and his worry about Gerdi and the others had been shovelled aside in the thrill of the pursuit.

"Okay, here goes," he said, and closed his eyes, taking a deep breath. Calica watched him. In the year since he had cracked the technique of controlling his power, back in Fane Aracq, he had become immeasurably more proficient in its use. Now that the huge destructive force he possessed had been harnessed, he could turn it to more subtle ends. No longer did he drain himself every time he unleashed his energy; in fact, he seemed to have virtually inexhaustible reserves. And he could do things now, subtle things. While she had been away, she'd heard tales of how he played the old Kirin board game of *jiriri* with his teacher Ogara-jin, never once touching the pieces.

*So long, we've been apart*, she thought, and felt a sudden and irrational desire to tell him then, to confess everything; how she felt for him, how she had inadvertently caused his mother's death, the whole story. But then there was a sudden clank from nearby, a great hiss of steam, and an outcry from the corridor as the cargo elevator jolted downwards.

"Go!" Ryushi cried, his eyes flicking open; and the two of them ran out into the firing line.

When the cargo elevator had started up, most of the Guardsmen had been too surprised to move. Some scrambled off it in time; all of the Jachyra did. One man hammered at the controls, trying to make the lift ascend again, but once it had started it could not be stopped. Of the forty Guardsmen, only ten or eleven were left to trouble Ryushi and Calica. Of the twenty Jachyra, each and every one came racing up the corridor towards them.

Ryushi threw a bolt of almost invisible energy out at them, sending it into the floor at their feet so that the explosive concussion would scatter them. Force-bolts slammed into him from the Guardsmen's halberds; but the protective bubble of his defences held strong against them, enclosing both him and Calica, who ran close by. They reached the service door as the Jachyra were leaping to their feet.

"Make it fast, Calica. I can't hold off that many Jachyra!" he urged, over the thick *wham* of the force-bolts as they impacted against his shield.

Calica set to work on the combination, and Ryushi turned his attention back to the Jachyra. They were too spaced out for a single assault to take them all, and he knew from experience how easily they could dodge smaller attacks. As they rushed towards him, finger-blades springing from their sheaths, he suddenly realized that he really *couldn't* hold them off, that if she didn't—

"Done," said Calica, as the door sprang open.

"That was fast," he said dumbly, a little surprised.

"Come *on*!" she cried, pulling him through and slamming the door behind them, a moment before the Jachyra reached the spot where they had been standing. The dials on the lock clicked back to their starting points again. They had a head start of the few dozen seconds it would take for the Jachyra to re-enter the code.

They ran down the service stairs, taking them two at a time and jumping the last few of each staircase, tearing recklessly round the corners. They could hear the loud grumbling of the cargo elevator near by, indicating that it was still on its way down. Above them, the door to the stairwell burst open and the Jachyra came swarming through.

And then the stairs ran out, and Calica slapped the palm-stud on the door at the bottom. They hurried through, pulling it closed behind them, but the Jachyra were already at the other side, frighteningly fast, and Ryushi swept his fist backwards into the lock mechanism of the door, adding just enough force from his spirit-stones to smash it irreparably.

"Will that hold them?" Calica asked, still running down the long rock corridor that led towards the mines.

"Should *I* know?" Ryushi replied, and a moment later a scatter of force-bolts hailed down on them, blasting a thin cloud of rock powder into the air. He glanced back over his shoulder and saw the cargo elevator settling to a halt a little way behind them, and the assembled Guardsmen pouring out.

Ryushi looked around desperately, caught in a moment of indecision. Destroying the rock corridor was not an option; he was underground now, he'd probably bring the whole mine down on their heads. Outrunning the Guardsmen was not much of a possibility either; they were close enough to fire, and Ryushi and Calica would certainly be hit many times over before they reached the other end of the long stretch to safety.

And then Ryushi's gaze fell on the rails at his feet, the twin set that ran from the cargo elevator all the way to buffers at the mouth of the disused tunnel where they had entered. And at the mine cart that rested in a lay-by a little way away.

He grabbed Calica's arm as they ran and pointed.

"You're not serious?" she said, her olive-green eyes narrowed in disbelief.

"Live a little, huh?" he said.

Another salvo of force-bolts peppered the air around them, smashing against Ryushi's defences or destroying sections of the tunnel. Ryushi barely noticed them, his whole attention fixed on the mine cart, a great, heavy thing of black iron. Already he was pushing against it, manipulating the invisible currents of energy in the air, knotting them behind the cart and urging it forward. It was reluctant at first, but it had been recently oiled and was in good condition, and after a few seconds it lurched into a slow trundle, heading away up the tunnel, gathering speed slowly.

Ryushi ducked through the hail of force-bolts and grabbed the side, pulling himself in. He reached out a hand to Calica, but she didn't need it, vaulting in after him and landing on her feet on the pebble-strewn floor of the cart. Calica looked back as the cart began to pick up speed, peering over the metal lip, and saw the door to the service stairs coming open and the Jachyra pouring through. The Guardsmen were running in pursuit, showering them with blasts from their halberds; but they were falling behind rapidly.

The Jachyra, however, were not. Running low, some of them going on all fours, they were not only keeping pace with the mine cart but actually *gaining* on it.

"Ryushi. . ."

"I know."

"The Jachyra!"

"I *know*!"

"So *step on it*!"

He did. With a yelp, Calica lost her footing and slid to the back of the cart, pressed to the metal with the force of the acceleration. Sparks sprayed from the wheels as they hit the junction where the lay-by met the main rails, and then they were hurtling down the mine tunnel, the Jachyra behind them slowing to a halt, hopelessly outpaced.

Calica clambered her way back to her feet. Ryushi was hunched over the front of the cart, his hair flapping about him and his clothes whipping around his arms and legs.

"Hey, slow *down*!" she cried, as they reached a long, slow curve to the left and she was thrown to the side of the cart again. Keeping one hand on the metal lip for support, she reached over and shook his shoulder. "We'll come off the rails!"

"Waaa-*hooo*!" he whooped, leaning forward as the cart tore around the bend at a speed that seemed certain to send them tumbling into the wall. "Don't worry about it, Calica. It's under control. Just enjoy the ride." He had a fierce grin on his face, that same look he sometimes had when he came back from a particularly exhilarating flight with Araceil. He'd always been reckless, but since Kia's death he had seemed to develop a taste for danger that bordered on addiction. There had been tales of things he'd done during the time when she was off searching for a way to deactivate the heartstone, tales that had worried her even then. His twin was dead, but it was as if he felt the need to reaffirm he was alive by throwing himself into any trouble he could find.

It was stupid, and terrifying; but when he was like this he seemed larger than life, and he practically glowed.

The cart slammed out of the curve and on to the long straight that ran across the huge rock bridge that spanned the first chamber they had come to. Calica's heart thudded in her chest, but she guessed that Ryushi was using a portion of his power to provide downforce, preventing the cart from derailing. She felt a flood of relief as she saw that the bridge was clear of other mine carts, but it soured a moment later as she saw the ur-Lan all across the vast cavern stopping their work and running to intercept them.

"I thought these guys were—"

"Maybe they've got orders to stop anyone coming through here when the alarm's going," Ryushi suggested, and Calica realized that she had forgotten the repetitive howl of the wind-siren, just as she had forgotten the bruise on her jaw dealt to her by Hochi. It had become part of the background noise in the thrill of the chase. "Doesn't matter, anyway. We'll just have to outrun them."

They were approaching the buffer at the far side of the bridge with frightening speed, the squat ur-Lan closing in on either side with their cannon-rams in their meaty hands. Calica knew that Ryushi was leaving it till the last minute to brake, to give them the maximum head start in the rush for daylight, but she still felt a grip on her chest squeeze tighter and tighter as he cut the margin finer and finer. . .

"Hang on," he said, and she did.

The deceleration was hard, so hard that they should by rights have been thrown out of the cart. But Ryushi's control over his power was greater than Calica had given him credit for; he cushioned the momentum for his passenger so that she felt nothing more than a moment of extreme terror. And then they were jumping out, hitting the ground at a run, the ur-Lan scrambling clumsily towards them with their brutal rock-drills wielded as weapons. They sprinted into the dark of the disused tunnel; Calica scrabbled a glowstone out of her pack as she ran, tossing off the rag that cloaked it, and they were surrounded by its orange light as they sprinted between the treacherous rocks and rubble that cluttered the floor before them.

The ur-Lan were slow, but they were relentless, and it was a long and exhausting run. When they finally reached the massive trapezoid gate that marked the entrance to the elevator shaft, they were on their last legs, and the bulky, low shapes of their pursuers were still clambering after them. Calica set the dials from memory and hit the palm-stud, and they ducked through the gate as it slid upwards. She hammered the button to close it behind them, and the gate switched direction mid-way through its opening sequence with a clank and a grinding noise. Finally, with a hiss, it settled into place, and there was silence, except for the laboured breathing of the two escapees as they rested against the rock wall.

"Ah-hah," Ryushi panted, half-laughing and half-gasping. "Ah-hah. That . . . felt good."

"You *idiot*!" Calica cried, hitting him on the arm. "You scared me to death!"

"Calica. . ."

"What?"

She didn't know what was happening for a few seconds; she was too surprised. All she knew was that suddenly, Ryushi's mouth was on hers, their lips sliding together, and they were kissing, deeply and desperately. The glowstone fell from her fingers and lay discarded on the floor, casting orange underlights on to the two figures that stood entwined in an embrace in the near-darkness, forgotten in the passion of the moment.

# 6

## A Counterpoint Cacophony

The temperature was near to unbearable. The sun pounded down on the sand, turning the curves of the dunes into a swelter of heat-haze. The cloudless sky was an endless field of perfect sapphire blue. Even the desert creatures took to the shade at midday, or burrowed into the cool earth. High in the sky, a paravane soared on the thermals, gliding towards its own den at the base of a distant butte. It was shaped like a hot-air balloon, with its small, round body and four symmetrically placed feet hanging beneath the inflated bulb of its leathery air sac. As it cruised through the sky, sheltered beneath its own shadow, its incurious eyes fell on the twin blotches on the smooth surface of the sand below.

Although it did not have the intelligence to

understand what the circumstances were, it had empathy enough to recognize a face-off when it saw one. On one side, a sprawling encampment, machines of black and grey iron arrayed around a multitude of tents and temporary constructions; on the other, across a great dip in the desert, standing on the crest of a long ridge of dunes, were thousands of warrior men and women, their swords glittering in the sun, on foot or krel-back, with the immense forms of the mukhili rising like islands from the sea of black-swathed humans.

Takami watched the paravane glide over their position, idly following its slow, steady progress across the sky. It was hot. Too hot for what he was wearing, the close-fitting, elegant green armour that had been a gift from Macaan upon delivering the information that had led to his family being executed. He had worn it when he had killed his father; he had worn it when Ryushi had taken his ear in his own court, and when he had been cheated of his victory by the Jachyra; and he wore it now, with a new silver mask fashioned in the effigy of a screaming spirit affixed around his face. The old one had disappeared one night from where he kept it in a cabinet. Heads had literally rolled before a replacement had been fashioned.

*Too hot. That's how they planned it. They can take the heat better than we can. They don't wear armour. Very clever. But where are the Sa'arin?*

A soldier joined him on the crest where he stood, making his way up from the disruptor post perimeter. He was wearing the desert-issue cream-white Guardsman armour. The standard black was impractical in these conditions – it was too heavy for walking across sand, and soldiers tended to overheat far too fast.

"What have you to report?" he said.

"This appears to be the extent of their army, my thane. Our scouts have reported no more forces approaching."

"And how did they *get* there without anyone noticing, Lieutenant?"

"We cannot say. The desert-folk know this terrain, and they are adept at covering their tracks, but . . . it seems they have assembled most, if not all of the tribes against us."

Takami glanced at his Lieutenant in disgust.

The soldier was clearly cowed by his superior. It was a reaction he had been getting more and more over the last year, since he had taken to wearing his mask all the time in public. The black, skin-tight material that pulled over his head like a balaclava served to disguise his mutilated left ear. So sometimes his temper following the marring of his countenance had been short enough to kill a few of his retainers for minor errors. So what? Surely fighting men would have a little more spine, even if their commander *was* renowned for killing those aides who displeased him. But the men Macaan had given him to make his assault on the desert were the very scrapings of the barrel, the most lax and disorganized of the Guardsmen. Conscripts, mostly; a lot of them without spirit-stones at all. Takami had long suspected he was being given a token force, intended to look more threatening than it actually was. A decoy, or bait.

Takami was silent, his face hidden behind the silver mask, blazing in the sun. "We have allowed them to choose the time of confrontation," he said. "They have the advantage. But we have the numbers, and the power."

"They got something else, too," said a voice from behind him. Takami remained where he was, still looking out over the army of desert-folk as the two newcomers joined them.

"Really?" he said blandly. "And what is that?"

"Old friend of yours," said Whist, ruffling the short neck hair of his massive dog, Blink. "They got Kia."

Li'ain sat under the shade of a small, light yellow canopy, one of the many that had been erected over the last hour. It was little more than a square of fabric stretched between four poles, but it served to mute the fury of the sun a little. Her skin had darkened in the six months she had spent in the desert, but not enough so that she could take the midday heat easily, even with the herbal paste she used to protect herself from burning. Behind her, final preparations were being made for the assault; but she was looking out over the desert, away from the battleground, to the gently shimmering horizon.

"Hey," Kia said, sitting down next to her.

Li'ain started.

"You alright?"

"Of course I am," Li'ain said, her fingers nervously pushing the strands of her long, onyx hair back into place. "What makes you think I—"

"Well, at first it was the way you were wringing your hands, then after that you started pouring sand through your fingers, then you started looking around at everyone and turning away if they caught your eye. . ." Kia said. "Anxious?"

Li'ain smiled timidly, and Kia was once again struck by how remarkably beautiful she was. "I have never been in a battle before," she admitted. "I am terrified."

Kia put a companionable arm around her. "You don't have to fight, y'know," she said. "This isn't your quarrel."

"It *is* . . . it *should* be," Li'ain replied. "Half a year I've been with these people, and they still don't treat me like one of them. Jedda's already said the same thing to me: *It is not your fight*. It makes me angry."

"You sound like you're *eager* to go into battle."

"No," she said. "I'd just like people to stop excusing me from it."

Kia sighed. "Seriously, Li'ain, what did you expect? Six months in the desert doesn't make you one of the desert-folk. You might be here six *years* and you'd still be an outlander. People don't just accept strangers like that; they don't just take them into the heart of their culture. I thought you might have learned that by now, unless you've been living on the moon all your life. One of them, anyway."

"Close enough," Li'ain muttered.

"Y'know," said Kia, leaning away from her a minute as if to get some distance to bring her into focus. "You strike me as someone who's a lot less worldly-wise than you first appear. There's no way you were born to this lifestyle. And your accent isn't any Dominion one I know."

"Maybe one day I will tell you," Li'ain replied, gazing out over the burning sea of sand.

Kia held her bo staff in her hands as a tightrope walker would hold a balance pole, testing its weight. It had suddenly turned up in her tent the night before; the very same one she had fought with at Base Usido. She suspected that Li'ain had more than a little to do with it. "Well, I still owe you one for getting me out of those mines, whatever your ulterior motives were. I'll look out for you out there. Unless I run into Takami."

"You hate him so much? Your own brother?"

"Oh, he stopped being my brother a long time ago," Kia said, getting to her feet. "They'll be attacking soon. We'd better get ready."

"Do you think Jedda was wise, choosing this time of day to fight? Will his *own* men be able to stand the heat?" Li'ain asked, walking with Kia out of the shade of the canopy, up the slope of a dune towards the line of desert warriors.

"If *they* can't, the Guardsmen certainly won't."

"He seems to have taken to you," Li'ain said, splitting off on another tangent.

"You think?" Kia laughed. "I doubt it."

"Desert-folk do not have red hair or green eyes," said Li'ain. "Your rarity makes you . . . desirable." When Kia gave her a strange look, she tilted her head and smiled. "I have learned *some* things during my time here."

"Are you trying to be a matchmaker?" Kia asked, vaguely amused.

Li'ain looked shocked, as if the thought had never occurred to her. "No, I – well, I was just—"

"It's alright, Li'ain. I appreciate the effort, but you're wasting your time," she sobered a little. "I lost Ty back in Kirin Taq. I don't want to replace him. I couldn't, if I tried."

"I apologize," said Li'ain, looking abashed. "I would just like you to be . . . happy."

Kia stopped, and Li'ain stopped with her. "Why?" she asked.

"Because. . ." the other began awkwardly, hesitated, then went on: "Because I would like to be your friend."

Kia felt a sudden urge to laugh, but she killed it before it could be born. It was such a mawkish, naïve thing to say; the kind of phrase used in stories but rarely in real life. The sort of thing that only children said, and adults wished they could. Once her initial amusement had faded, she found it almost unbearably charming, as if Li'ain had reverted to an adorable infant in front of her eyes. It reminded her of Elani, when she was not being mature beyond her years.

"Li'ain," she said, with as much gravity as she could muster. "You *are* my friend. You might have your secrets, but you've done nothing but help me out since you found me. I don't know what I did to deserve you."

She was surprised and a little embarrassed to see Li'ain's eyes fill with tears. "Do you really mean that?"

"Of course I do," Kia said, hugging her. "Hey, don't worry. You're just strung out because of this fight. You'll be okay."

"Thank you," Li'ain whispered.

*Am I worth that much to her?* Kia thought. *She's a whole lot more complex than she seems.*

They parted, and Li'ain sheepishly wiped the tears from her eyes. "I apologize. I am embarrassing you."

"'S okay. You ready?"

She nodded. "I think I am."

The attack began shortly after.

It was unusually organized to Kia's eyes, more like a joust than a battle. Her experience of mass combat had always involved sneak attacks, surprises, ambushes. But this was the desert; even with all the stealth the nomads could muster, they would not be able to get close enough to gain much of an advantage before they were seen. It seemed absurd, that the two forces should be so civilized about something so uncivilized as war; that Takami's camp should allow the desert-folk to assemble on one side of the sand-valley, and that the desert-folk should do the same for their opponents. If Takami's forces had mobilized immediately upon sighting the approaching nomads, their enemies would have been more spread out, disorganized and vulnerable; if the desert-folk had attacked in a charge rather than forming up into a makeshift camp, Takami would have had no time to bring his war-machines into play.

But neither did, and so they stood, facing off. Until the sun reached its zenith, and the high-pitched horns of the desert-folk shrieked. From Takami's camp, wind-sirens howled in response and the two sides boiled over the sides of the valley and spilled down the shallow slopes to fight.

The armies spread into layers as they charged, like liquids of different densities separating out in water. The front line of both sides were the krel, loping ahead of the rest of the army. The desert-folk riders shook their weapons at the air and yelled battle-cries; the Guardsmen, in their off-white armour, held their halberds ready and swept in to meet them at the bottom of the dip. Behind the riders were the foot-soldiers, those who could not ride or did not have mounts; and behind them were the heavy weapons.

One of the most crucial problems in any attempt to conquer the tribes of the desert was the desert itself. Though much of the terrain was hard, stony soil, a large proportion of the inner reaches was soft, deep sand, such as they fought on now. Moving weighty machinery around on such a surface was almost impossible, and usually more trouble than it was worth. The standard war-machines sank into the sand and got stuck there, or their mechanisms became clogged with grit. Perhaps, given time, a solution might have been found; a way to overcome this problem. But the desert invasion had never been a priority with Macaan, so it had never been properly addressed.

It evened the odds somewhat. For the Guardsmen, there were force-cannons mounted on tracked platforms, light enough to traverse the dunes, and Sidewinders – the long, serpentine metal caterpillars that were the only specialized vehicles for desert warfare. For the nomads, there were the massive mukhili, their lumpy black carapaces swarming with archers and warriors, swathed in loose black robes.

The front lines of the two sides clashed hard in a roar of sound as the tide of krel met and melted together, the black of the desert-folk and the white of the Guardsmen. Scimitars blazed as the light caught them, clashing with halberds or cutting through armour. Unlike standard Guardsman attire, the lighter desert issue was thin enough to be breached by a blade, if swung hard enough. The nomads exploited the fact without mercy.

"They're not firing!" said Kia, from her vantage point. "Why aren't the Guardsmen firing?"

She was standing on one of the great wood-and-rope gantryways that hung against one side of a mukhili that was jolting downward towards the battle below. Like the others, the rough dome of its back was covered with a series of small platforms, walkways and howdahs that were secured by huge bolts driven into the creature's exoskeleton. They were all interconnected with ropes, and most were designed to flex with the juddering of the mukhili's movement; but because the carapace was all in one piece, like the shell of a tortoise, it was reasonably stable.

With Kia was Li'ain. Jedda was up near the vast, flattish head of the creature, from which its black eyes and huge mandibles protruded. He was a mukhili rider, like many Rai'kel, with the spirit-stones in his back that enabled him to tame the enormous insects. It was the same principle as with the Bonding-stone that Kia owned, a present from her father that had disappeared somewhere along the way, presumably taken by the Overseer of Osa'ara mines when she had been bought. She had found it again in her cell a short time later. Another piece of her past lost and regained. She didn't care anymore. Souvenirs of her life were too transient and fragile, gone too easily. She had learned that with Ty. She wouldn't place her trust in one again.

"They should be using their halberds," Kia said again, this time more to herself than to anyone else. "Something's wrong."

Li'ain stood next to her, her hands tight on the edge of the gantryway. "Maybe they don't want to drain themselves too early," she said, her voice small.

"You sure you're up to this?" said Kia.

Li'ain drew a long, slender blade from her scabbard and looked along its length. "I have to be," she said.

The mukhili ploughed into the fray, smashing through Guardsmen, gathering the enemy up in their cruel mandibles and cracking them like eggs. The desert-folk had purposely left areas of the battlefield undefended so that the mukhili could break through the ranks and surge into the heart of the Guardsmen, without killing their own people on the way. Li'ain held tighter to the side of the gantryway as the mukhili bucked and rocked, and then suddenly the air around them was cut with the *whoosh* of arrows as the archers opened up on the people below. A moment later, the thick *whump* of force-bolt fire began – the small, rapid reports of the Guardsmen's halberds and the bigger, slower hits of the mobile artillery.

"There are your force-cannons," said Li'ain.

Kia was distracted, half her mind on gathering up the abseiling ropes at their feet and securing them to their belts and the other half on the battle below. "It's only the back ranks that are firing. You think the ones at the front can't fire?"

"Macaan has been recruiting," Li'ain said. "Some of the conscripts do not have stones."

"Conscripts?" Kia said, standing up, surprise on her face. "Then Macaan's been dragging *more* people into his war?"

Li'ain made no reply, but her silence was answer enough. Kia cursed. Conscripts. These were not people who had been indoctrinated since infancy, like most Guardsmen were. Them, she had never had any problem with killing; they were the fists of Macaan, his disciples. Though they had been taken from their parents, given no choice, she believed them lost already by the time they were old enough to fight. But conscripts . . . they were Dominion-folk, who thought and acted as Dominion-folk did, and who had been brought into a war they did not want to fight.

"I wish you hadn't told me that," she said, checking their ropes. All along the gantryway, other warriors were getting ready. Li'ain peered nervously over the edge of the mukhili. It was a long way down to the bloodied sand below, where the nomads were leaping over the corpses of the fallen to fight savagely with the enemy. This mukhili, like the others that the nomads had, was intended to carry a force deep into the heart of the fighting and then deposit them there. It was the way of the desert-folk; break up the organization of the enemy, make them uncertain, destroy their discipline. Nomads worked far better independently than trained soldiers did.

Li'ain wiped the sweat from her brow. The tanned skin of her bare arms glistened with it. She looked at Kia, who was wearing light travel clothes borrowed from her own chest; Kia smiled reassuringly at her. For a moment, an unbearable temptation seized her: *This is not your fight, you do not have to do this, you are not one of them.*

She choked it off before it could take her over, in the only way she could think of. With her rappelling line in one hand, sword in the other, she vaulted over the edge of the gantryway and dropped to the battle below.

# 7

## Moments of Chaos

It was like descending into a nightmare.

Li'ain thumped down on top of a Guardsman who was rushing to get out of the way of the mukhili's huge flanks, bearing him down to the ground as her legs buckled and she fell on top of him. He thrashed beneath her, trying to get his unwieldy halberd between them, but something had wedged it and he was unable to pull it free. She drew back her slender sword, the point aimed at the crevice between the Guardsman's helmet and breastplate. . .

. . .and could not bring herself to drive it home.

The Guardsman, seeing her hesitation, suddenly clamped his hands around the wrist of her sword arm, twisting it hard so that she would drop her weapon. She might have done so, had not Kia suddenly crashed down from above, ramming the end of her bo staff into the Guardsman's armoured jaw with all the momentum of her fall behind it. He jerked and went limp.

"Like *that*," she said, pulling Li'ain to her feet. "You do know how to use that sword, don't you?"

"Jedda . . . gave me some lessons," Li'ain panted, fear making her short of breath.

Kia muttered an oath of disbelief. "You'd better stick *real* close."

More desert-warriors landed all about them now. The mukhili was staying still on purpose, under Jedda's guidance, while the fighters spilled from its immense flanks. Against the mountainous creature, Li'ain felt like an ant in its presence; she was relieved when the knot of dark-swathed warriors began to push away from it, their scimitars sweeping as they forged into the heart of the action. Force-cannons thudded from the enemy camp, bending the air with invisible bolts, producing an effect not unlike the heat-haze of the desert. It was swelteringly, chokingly hot amid the press of bodies, and the air was stifling and smelled of blood baking in the sun.

Kia jostled Li'ain to the centre of the slowly expanding clot of desert-folk, keeping her protected as much as she could. Why she had insisted on joining the battle, Kia had no idea; but inexperienced as she was, she was a liability to herself and others. Kia kept half an eye on her as she jabbed and darted with her staff, beads of sweat flying from her bare skin, sending lethal strikes between the ranks of the nomads, but Li'ain appeared to be distracted, looking for something.

"Li'ain! Watch your right!" she cried suddenly, as a Guardsman slashed aside a broad-shouldered ox of a nomad and broke through the ranks. Li'ain was directly in his path. She looked up at Kia's cry, her eyes widening in alarm, her sword coming up instinctively to block the down-swing of the blade. Kia leaped towards her, knowing she would be too late, the Guardsman had come out of nowhere, and Li'ain's parry was far too weak to stop the halberd. . .

The two edges of metal met, there was a sharp pulse of something, some energy that Kia was too surprised to define . . . and the Guardsman's armour clattered to the ground. His armour, and

113

*only* his armour; for the person inside it had disappeared without trace.

Kia stared as Li'ain turned to look at her, her sleek black hair damp with sweat and strung across her face. She opened her mouth to speak, but she was cut off by the screech of a signal-rocket that flew into the sky from the enemy camp, high up on the crest of a dune. It terminated in a rude staccato splutter of explosions, making Li'ain look up.

"That's it!" she said excitedly. "That's the signal!"

"What signal?" Kia cried.

"You want to get to Takami? You want to get into the enemy camp?" she asked, running over to her, pushing through the fighters that surrounded them.

"What's this all about, Li'ain? "Course I do!"

"Then just trust me," she said. "Watch my back."

She raised her hand to the clear sky and from it burst a pillar of energy, boiling slashes of green and black that swirled around each other as they tore up to the heavens. Kia fended off the attack of a Guardsman, who was trying to make his way through the nomads to get to them, then turned around and shouted over her shoulder.

"Li'ain! What are you *doing*?"

"Hold on to me!" she urged, cutting off the pillar and letting it streak away into the sky. There was a slight shift in the air pressure, noticeable even in the sweltering heat and frantic activity of the battle. Li'ain grabbed Kia's arm as the Parakkan turned around and came face to face with a figure she had thought – and hoped – she would never see again.

"Hey Kia," said Whist. "Long time no see."

And with that he took Li'ain's hand; the other one he laid on the back of his enormous canine companion, and the chain was complete. Blink, Whist, Li'ain, and Kia; all disappeared, as if they had never been there.

Takami stood amid a circle of bodyguards, watching the battle rage across the valley below. The desert-folk were doing well, better than could have been expected against an army of Guardsmen. But then, calling these slow-brained idiots *Guardsmen* was something of an undeserved compliment. He seethed with anger behind the emotionless exterior of his mask. They were *decoys*, sword-fodder, just there to soak up the numbers and give the desert-folk something to chew on while Macaan got on with his business in the Machinists' Citadel. The wyverns that had been part of the army that conquered the Citadel had supposedly been despatched to aid the desert forces, but they had never arrived. Most likely, Macaan had simply spread the rumour so that his generals did not ask where they *really* were. Probably engaged in another fruitless decoy, like he was.

*What is that regal fool doing?*

It wasn't only him who was losing faith in Macaan. He could see it in the eyes of the nobles at court, and he heard it in the voices of the gossips. Nobody dared *say* it, but everyone knew what everyone else was thinking. Macaan had got reckless since Aurin died. He threw his forces about here and there with no thought for the tactics and strategy that had made him such a mighty leader in the first place. Reports that the

Parakkan counter-invasion had started only made things worse. There was talk of a plan, some kind of secret that Macaan had up his sleeve, that would annihilate Parakka for good . . . but who in the courts believed that?

*All I know,* he thought bitterly, *is that he's ordered me to attack south. He's condemned me here to die with the scum of his army just to buy him some time.*

He should just leave. Take a wyvern – there were a few, including his own personal mount – and go. But where was there left for him? He could only go back to Macaan.

And there was one thing for him to do first. Somehow the desert-folk had pacified the Sa'arin. Was it a coincidence that Kia had returned from the dead at almost exactly the same time? He didn't think so.

His cursed siblings. Ryushi had taken his ear and killed his benefactor, Aurin. Kia had helped to thwart his invasion of Base Usido, and was now contributing to what would be his second failure. He was angry, and the anger needed venting on something.

"Prepare a Sidewinder," he said through gritted teeth. "I'm going down there."

"—ist! You son of a—" Kia said as they rematerialized, then stopped as the disorientation from the sudden, unexpected jump set in. She pulled herself away from Li'ain, unsteady on her feet, trying to size up her surroundings. Bright; somewhere outside. Tents around, and metal crates and—

"Love to stay, Kia, but you'd probably try 'n' kill me," Whist said with a roguish grin, before planting a swift kiss on her lips and winking out again.

Kia swore, wiping her mouth with the back of her hand, and concentrated on breathing steadily for a few seconds until her head stopped swimming and found its level again.

She was alone. Whist's cursed Flicker Dog had taken both him and Li'ain with it when it disappeared. She didn't even know he could *do* that; she never expected Blink to be able to transport other people on his jumps, in the same way that Elani could when she shifted. She owed

Whist a big payback for betraying her not once but twice on Os Dakar; she owed him double for duping Ryushi later on and leading him into Takami's clutches, something that Calica had told her about.

What did Li'ain have to do with him? It was clear that the firework from the camp was a signal, and that Li'ain's pillar of energy had been intended as a beacon, to guide Whist to where they were. The two were working together. And Li'ain had lied about her spirit-stones. She'd said she was a Fetch, with the power to steal things over long distances. But the power she had wielded was phenonemal; Kia had felt the energy backlash. She was no Fetch, if such a thing even existed.

So who was Li'ain? And *who* had been delivering those little presents to her in the mines?

No time to think now. What had she said? *You want to get to Takami?* A quick glance around confirmed her suspicions; she was inside the enemy camp, hidden amid stacks of boxes and empty storage bins that were heaped up between two pavilion tents. Peering out, she saw the sand fall away into a shallow dip, which was sheltered under an immense canopy. A makeshift vehicle bay lay there, where two mobile force-cannons and three Sidewinders sat idle, being serviced by the maintenance personnel that ran about in the shade. Just beyond that was a dune crest, where a cluster of people stood watching the battle below.

Would Takami be there? She squinted to see, but the glare of the blinding sun on the white sand rendered the soldiers silhouettes. From the other side of the ridge, the sounds of battle raged, and Kia felt almost guilty that she had been plucked from the fray. Her mind flitted to Jedda for some reason; she brought it harshly back to the situation at hand.

Whist had brought her here for a purpose. Takami? Probably. She looked closer at the group of people watching the battle. Other soldiers, messengers most likely, ran up to them periodically, spending a moment with them before disappearing again. Giving reports and relaying orders. Yes, that was the command alright, or a section of it. Takami *had* to be there.

She turned her attention to the Sidewinders,

searching out possible cover for her approach. They were long, segmented things, tapering towards the tail, with their "heads" being the biggest part of them. This foremost section was covered with a smooth, domed blast-shield through which cockpit windows stared like eyes in some bizarre cross between a fish and an eel. The other segments had small, swivelling force-cannons in their flanks. She had seen them in action, from the back of the mukhili. They moved with a strange side-to-side shimmying motion to spread their weight; otherwise they might drive themselves into a trench of their own making, in the soft desert sand. It made their guns inaccurate, but the sheer number of them more than made up for it.

As she watched, one was being prepared. Artillerists were boarding it, their usual green armour replaced by a paler shade to reflect the heat. She was about to break cover and skirt around the edge of the open-air vehicle bay when her eye fell on one of the silhouettes from atop the crest. It was making its way down towards the bay, striding with some purpose.

She squinted again, motivated by some instinct she did not recognize. Something about this one. . .

He stepped into the shade, and the glare from his armour receded, and she saw.

Takami.

"Is everything ready?" he asked the Guardsman who waited for him by the entrance hatch in the flank of the vehicle.

"The Sidewinder is prepared, my thane. But do you really think it is wise to—"

"No, I don't," he replied sharply, and left it at that. He stepped in through the curving rectangle of the hatchway and went inside. The Guardsman was about to shut it when he spotted an Artillerist hurrying over to him.

"Get inside, you idiot!" he hissed. "Takami'll skin you if he notices you're late." And get a uniform that fits, he added mentally, noticing the outfit was too broad across the shoulder. Artillerists were always a little eccentric; it came with the job of firing force-cannons endlessly. The sound had to get to them after a while.

The Artillerist stepped inside and went to the tail of the craft. The hatch was in one of the foremost sections, but not actually at the head. That was where Takami had gone. The newcomer went the other way.

It was cramped and hot and dark inside the belly of the Sidewinder. There was barely room to squeeze past the other Artillerists who sat in their tiny metal seats and peered out through peepholes that cast horizontal slits of light across their eyepieces. The newcomer took the vacant gun and sat in it.

Several dozen metres away, behind a stack of metal storage bins and crates, the sand stirred and shifted, revealing the knuckles of a bare hand.

Kia's heart thudded in her chest, the insistent percussion of the nervous fear that charged her body. She'd been forced to leave her bo staff behind when she adopted her disguise, burying it with the body of the unfortunate Artillerist using the power of her spirit-stones. Now she was weaponless – except for the pitiful short sword that was the standard issue of the Artillerists – and trapped within the stifling armour of Macaan's gunners. It was hard to breathe behind the visor in this kind of temperature.

But it would be worth it, she told herself. She wasn't letting Takami get away from her.

There was a rapidly ascending hum as the Sidewinder's Pilot powered it up, drawing energy from the earth through his spirit-stones and forcing it into the mechanisms of the vehicle. Kia felt tears suddenly threaten her eyes, absurdly reminded of Ty by the sound.

*Forget him, he's gone*, she told herself cruelly. She thought of Takami, and her tears dried.

"She got on *that*?" Whist cried. "What is *with* that family? Are they *all* nuts?"

Li'ain crouched next to him in the shade of a tall, long tent, fixed in the soft sand by anchor-poles. There was little activity in the camp while the battle was being fought down below, and it was not hard for them to remain unseen as they watched Kia from higher up the slope of one of the great dunes. She had watched in silence as Kia had lured and killed the Artillerist and boldly climbed aboard the Sidewinder. Now her eyes followed it as it curved out of the camp, down towards the combat.

"She is out of the way," Li'ain said. "It was what we intended, eventually; she has just done it earlier than we thought. Now she is on her own. She can handle herself."

"Yeah, no kidding," said Whist. "So what now?"

"It would be best if you left. I have to carry out the rest of the plan."

"Don't worry, I'm gone," he replied, absently patting Blink. Blink whuffed and scratched his ear with a hind leg. "Just curious, is all. Why *are* you doing all this? You sweet on that Jedda guy or what?"

She smiled faintly. "No, Whist. I just have to clear a debt," she said.

Whist gave her an odd look, his painted features furrowing beneath the multi-coloured thatch of his hair. "Okay, whatever. I'll catch up with you later."

Li'ain took the hand that was encased in a metal glove in both of hers. "Thank you, Whist," she said, sincerely.

For a moment he paused, and something threateningly close to a genuine emotion passed over his face. Then he pulled away with a snort. "I dunno *why* I'm doing this," he said, and he and Blink disappeared, leaving her alone.

Li'ain looked at the spot where he and his omnipresent companion had been for a few seconds, before switching from a crouch to a kneeling position, relaxing herself with several deep breaths. It was burning hot, even in the shade, and she did not know how well the herbal paste that glistened on her skin would protect her. She ignored the discomfort, closing her eyes, searching for the Flow, for the ley lines that ran beneath the desert.

Slowly, inexorably, the hum of power began to build around her.

The Sidewinder tore down the slope and on to the battlefield. The sand – previously smooth – had become a torrid churn of grit and blood. The lighter, unarmoured desert warriors had been fighting on familiar terrain, while the Guardsmen were both less experienced at combat and wearing cumbersome suits that dragged them down into the soft ground. The tactic of fighting at high noon was paying off now; some of Takami's forces were fainting from heatstroke or lack of oxygen as they fought, and the rest were flagging fast. The mukhili were cutting devastating swathes through the enemy; they had already caught and crushed several Sidewinders in their massive mandibles. The mobile force-cannons still rained bolts down on the fighters, but most of those Guardsmen with the ability to fire their halberds – which Takami had been keeping back to use as archers – had been scattered by a brave push from the desert-folk, and had entered the fray in hand-to-hand combat.

Takami had manned the turret gun of the Sidewinder, occupying a spot just behind the Pilot's seat. He sat hunched over a periscope, which was linked to the flat, swivelling cannon just behind the head section of the vehicle, a specially modified weapon for his own personal use. He did not have the blue stones of force that the Guardsmen and Ryushi had; but with a few minor modifications, the gun had been adapted to focus his own spirit-stones, the green and amber stones that generated his ethereal fire.

They entered the fray, crashing heedlessly into friend and foe alike, and the gunners opened up, sowing force-bolts either side of them. Takami swivelled in his seat, left and right, his green armour darkened to a murky yellow-black in the orange light of the interior glowstones. Beneath his mask, a fierce grin spread across his face, and when he finally fired he cried out in exultation. He'd really *needed* this.

From high up above the battle, in the howdah on the back of his mukhili, Jedda and his massive mount turned as one towards the Sidewinder as Takami fired. The great ball of green fire streaked across the battlefield, into a thick mass of nomads, and exploded with enormous force, incinerating them where they stood. When the smoke cleared, there was only a charred and blackened dent in the sand, surrounded by the writhing figures of those who had been burned on the periphery of the explosion.

"Go!" Jedda cried, seeing the immediate danger, and urged his mukhili towards it.

Takami was not aware of the commotion behind him. The noise of the Sidewinder's mechanisms and the roar of the battle all around swamped the sound of clattering. He did not even notice the guns along the flank of the Sidewinder going silent. His attention was focused on the mukhili that had suddenly begun to lumber towards him, filling his viewer. *They* were what were keeping the desert-folks' hopes alive. Without them, nothing could threaten the Sidewinders. And wouldn't it be satisfying to see one of those huge things blow apart? Maybe Kia was even on it.

*Kia*. He had almost forgotten, in the heat of his need to kill, why he had entered the battle in the first place. Since his mutilation by Ryushi, since his fine good looks had been marred for ever, he had found that his frustration at the world could only be sated by murder. *He had made the wrong choice*. He shouldn't have betrayed his family, shouldn't have sided with Macaan because

Parakka were gaining the edge, and Macaan was losing it fast.

On the other hand, if he hadn't, then his siblings would not have become such a thorn in Macaan's side, Ryushi would not have killed Aurin, and Parakka might have been wiped out. He couldn't win.

But he could find his sister. And kill *her*. That was the least he could do.

*First, this little problem*, Takami thought. He aimed at the mukhili's head, squaring the crosshair right between its dark, soulless insect eyes.

"Hey bro. Remember me?" came the voice at his shoulder, cold with menace.

The shot and his reaction to his sister's voice came at the same moment. He swivelled around in his chair, but the energy that had already been released from his spirit-stones was too far gone on its journey to call back. On the inside, Takami jerked round and out of his chair to face his sister; on the outside, a new blast of energy spat from the Sidewinder's cannon, trailing curls of flame through the air, smashing into the mukhili dead-on. . .

. . .and dissipating.

Jedda felt the immense surge of pain and anger from the mukhili beneath him, linked as they were through their Bonding-stones. He flinched and cried out in sympathetic agony as the energy hit them. He had no way of knowing that, if Takami had not been distracted, then the full force of the bolt would have turned his mount to a pile of steaming, scorched guts and a jigsaw of chitin armour. But the mukhili had been hurt, and creatures such as they were not used to being hurt. Rage swamped it, and swamped Jedda, too. Heedless of the warriors that still occupied the howdahs and walkways strung across its carapace, it broke into a thundering charge, heading for the thing that had hurt it – the Sidewinder in which Takami and Kia now met for the first time since Osaka Stud had been destroyed.

Kia held the point of her short sword beneath the jawline of Takami's mask, pressing it into his flesh. A runnel of sweat made its way from his skin down the cool steel of the Artillerist's blade.

"Don't even think about trying your stones," she warned.

At the very front of the Sidewinder, the Pilot looked back over his shoulder, noticing that Takami was not firing any more. The vehicle stuttered and jolted as he saw the scene behind him. The narrow, cramped metal tunnel of the Sidewinder's body was littered with Artillerists, either unconscious or dead. Standing before Takami was a red-haired girl, wearing an Artillerist's armour from the neck down, her sword at Takami's throat.

"Keep driving," she snarled at him. "Get us away from the battle."

Pilots were not fighters, and he carried no weapon. He nodded in frightened agreement and turned back to his controls.

Just in time to see the enormous frame of the mukhili bearing down on them.

With a cry, he slammed the Sidewinder into a hard right turn, stamping the brakes to steepen the angle. Kia and Takami were both flung back and sideways against the interior of the craft, smacking hard into the metal curve of the Sidewinder's entrance hatchway. Kia's sword caught and twisted on something, wrenching hard out of her grip, and Takami fell on top of her, crushing her to the floor with his weight, his hands already reaching for her throat.

But the Pilot's emergency manoeuvre had not been enough to pull them out of the way of the mukhili. It thundered towards them as they sped across the battlefield, grinding corpses beneath them and knocking aside the living.

"Oh, little *sister*," Takami breathed, the swell of Flow racing through his stones, ready to unleash his fire through the hands that held Kia's throat. "You really *shouldn't* have made it so easy."

"You always were . . . too cursed arrogant," she gasped. "I got you right where I want you."

Takami began to laugh, but his laugh faded as Kia suddenly lashed out with her hand, thumping the palm-stud next to the entrance hatchway. In the blink of an eye, two things happened at once: there was a loud hiss as the door slid open; and Kia pulled her feet under Takami's chest and rolled backwards. Takami cried out in surprise and alarm as the two of them were carried out of the speeding vehicle. There was a moment of sickening weightlessness, and then they both hit the sand, far harder than either of them had expected. Chaos followed as their unstoppable momentum rolled and threw them along the sand, flinging them into the legs of the Guardsmen and nomads that fought in desperate clusters all around them.

Kia had barely stopped rolling, bruised all over, when nomad hands reached down and helped her to her feet, recognizing the bright red of her hair even with the Artillerist uniform on. "Takami!" she shouted as a challenge, casting about frantically, even though her vision was still blurred and she was dizzy. To her right, there was the huge lunge of the mukhili, as it snapped up the Sidewinder they had fallen out of and lifted it in the air, crushing it between its vicious mandibles.

"*Takami!*" she shrieked again, but it was no use. He had disappeared into the battle, lost in the crowd.

Behind them, there was a sudden, almighty eruption, the concussion of the blast stirring their hair even where they stood. As one, every combatant looked up at the crest of the dune where Takami's camp was, in time to see the vast, shrieking pillar of seething green and black energy expand outward from a single point, becoming larger and larger until it had consumed everything around it in its deafening noise and turbulence.

And then, as suddenly as it began, it quietened. A great hush descended. Where the camp had been, there was nothing; only an immense blast-pattern in the sand. And there, kneeling in the centre of the destruction, a tiny figure.

"Li'ain," Kia said in disbelief.

After that, the battle was merely a formality. Most of the Guardsmen gave up immediately; they were conscripts, who did not want to fight, and their fear of execution by their officers was outweighed by their reluctance to die for a King they hated. A few isolated pockets of Guardsman resistance refused to surrender; but without their mobile force-cannons or any chain of command, they were lost. The nomads sensed their victory long before it arrived; and the final mopping-up was done with almost cheery good humour.

Kia searched through the battlefield, stepping between the hacked and mangled bodies of the dead. She had long since become numbed to such sights. This was war, after all. The losses had been terrible on both sides, but somehow, she could not bring herself to feel more than a vague sense of sorrow and tragedy.

*Takami was not there.*

However he had escaped, he was not among the dead.

*Takami was not there.*

She ran her hand through her hair and felt tears of hot anger and frustration prick at her eyes.

*Takami.*

# 8

## The Eventual Hope of Unity

A new temporary camp had been set up, near to the battlefield, where the wounded could be treated. It was night, and the temperature had plummeted, but the nomad healers worked on by lamplight. The desert was a cool, dark ocean, shrouding the evidence of the carnage that had occurred in soft folds of twilight. The moons were out in the clear sky; the petite blue sphere of Mauni hiding within the frame of its huge, mottled white sister, Cetra.

Kia walked between the tents, Jedda with her. She found a strange comfort in his presence, even when he was silent; he radiated a calm and strength that reassured her somehow. She was dressed in furs, he in several layers of heat-retaining fabrics to combat the chill. Their boots scuffed the sand as they walked.

"You will find your brother," he said after a time.

"Which one?" Kia asked rhetorically.

He answered anyway. "Both," he said. "We are moving north tomorrow. Towards your homeland. Messengers have been despatched to the Noman tribes in the steppes."

"They didn't listen before," said Kia.

"They may listen to us. We are nomads, like them; never underestimate the power of a common bond. You do not want to know what many of our folk think of your cities."

She laughed. "I'm sure the reverse is true, as well."

"You want to ask about Li'ain, don't you?"

"I was getting round to it," Kia admitted. "You know who she is? I mean *really*?"

"No," he replied. "No, I do not. But we all have our secrets."

"Well, she's gonna level with me when she wakes up," Kia said. "Anyone working with Whist has got to be—"

"Be kind to her," Jedda urged, interrupting. "She did a great thing today. She won the battle for us, but it has drained her. She needs a few days to recover."

"It'll take that long to get to where we're going."

"You know a place?"

"Oh yeah. You heard of Gar Jenna?"

"The secret base of Parakka. Of course."

"We'll go there. Just you and me. That's where we'll find out what's going on."

"And Li'ain?"

"We'll see," Kia said.

Jedda laughed suddenly. "Ah, already you have taken charge. I knew Li'ain was not wrong, when she told me about you. You placated the Sa'arin; now you will lead us to Parakka." He took her hand suddenly, in both of his. "You are a marvel, Kia," he said, looking into her eyes.

She felt a flush at his touch, sudden and unexpected. At first, it was warm and wonderful, and as she searched his face she saw in his dark-skinned features something she had only ever seen in Ty's before; and then an ugly wash of guilt spread through her, and she gently pulled her hand away.

"You must have loved him dearly," Jedda said, reading truth into her reaction.

"I don't know," she whispered, seeming to diminish in front of him. "I don't know if I did."

She did not add the rest of the sentence that completed itself in her mind against her will: *because if I* did *love him, it never felt half as strong as what I feel for you.*

"I must . . . tell the Sa'arin what has happened today," she said, and hurried away. He stayed where he was, and watched her go, and then turned and walked back the way they had come, towards where Li'ain lay.

"Get up. You're being moved," said the Guardsman.

Gerdi looked up from where he sat in the corner of the featureless, dingy metal cell at the figure who stood silhouetted in the doorway. Hochi did not react.

"Where we going?" Gerdi asked wearily.

"You'll know when you get there. Now move."

Gerdi got to his feet, scratching at the Damper Collar that chafed his neck. The single, white Damper stone set into it effectively deactivated his powers of illusion. Hochi got up also. He had been given no collar.

Gerdi watched his adopted guardian's back as they were led in single file, with a Guardsman in front and behind, down the dim, dank corridors of the holding pens in the depths of the Machinists' Citadel. The feeble striplights crackled and flickered as they passed underneath them. The air was cold and smelt of oil. Where Quain had been taken, they had no idea.

All this time. All this time, and Gerdi had never known, until their captors broke one of the greatest taboos of the Dominions. Hochi had been unwilling to be meekly led to his imprisonment when he had been caught in the laboratory where he had been left by Ryushi and Calica. The Guardsmen had subdued him, but not before his simple shirt had ripped and come free. He was taken to Gerdi's cell bare from the waist up, and that was when Gerdi found out.

It was unthinkable to ask another person about the properties of their spirit-stones, much less forcibly reveal them against their will. It was an individual's personal choice to reveal or conceal the gifts of their *pah'nu'kah*. Socially, it prevented people judging each other on the generosity or affluence of their parents; spirit-stones were an incredibly expensive commodity. It was just . . . *not done.* Gerdi had lived with Hochi for many winters, and had no reason to be suspicious. People often had stones that were not used for decades – the white and red stones of regeneration, for instance, that only came into effect when the host was badly wounded.

Hochi didn't have *any* stones.

Even someone as flighty as Gerdi, for whom depth of insight was a rare and alien thing, understood what that meant. In a world where everyone except the poorest or most unfortunate of people had some special ability or another through their stones, it was a crippling blow. Blacksmiths could shape metal beneath their hands, but a blacksmith without stones would fare badly against his competitors, no matter how skilled he was. It was the same in any profession; to lack stones was a huge disadvantage.

And Hochi had become the head of a thriving wyvern stud in Tusami City, as well as a respected and valued member of Parakka, who impressed everyone with his boundless courage and endurance and his generous heart . . . And all the time, he had done it without a single stone on his back.

Gerdi would never have admitted it, but he was achingly proud of his guardian.

They were taken to a new cell, the same size as the one they had left and in all respects identical, except for one thing; there were other people in it.

"Orders," said the lead Guardsman curtly, to the two figures inside. "You're getting some company."

They hustled Gerdi and Hochi inside, and closed the cell door behind them with a clang. There were the sounds of receding footsteps, then silence. For a long moment, the newcomers peered into the gloom. The cell was even dimmer than the corridor, barely lit at all. In the shadows, the two figures that occupied the cell stirred.

"Uncle Hochi?" came a small voice.

"*Elani?*" Hochi cried, rushing over to the tiny figure. Gerdi blinked in surprise; it was the most overt display of emotion he had seen from the man for a long time. For a moment, the two regarded each other in disbelief. Then Hochi swept up the tiny Resonant girl in his arms, hugging her fiercely, and she threw her own slender arms around his neck. Tears flowed down both their faces as Hochi spun her into the faint light from the cell window, the child who, like Gerdi, he had been guardian over for a time, and whom he had thought was dead.

"Oh, I'm so happy to see you both," came the voice from the other occupant of the cell, and from the shadow stepped the tall, lithe form of Peliqua, her ash-grey skin blending with the darkness, her hands clasped together before her chest. She made to hug Gerdi, but he took a step back with a warning glare, and she smiled, remembering how uncomfortable he was with displays of affection. Hochi released Elani and embraced the Kirin girl, and Elani ignored Gerdi's preferences and hugged him anyway. He squirmed a little before reluctantly returning the hug.

They sat down together on the hard metal floor, and exchanged more greetings and exclamations of happiness before Hochi finally brought them up short by saying:

"Elani, Peliqua. What have they *done* to you?"

Gerdi had not noticed in the darkness of the cell, but as his vision adjusted he saw what Hochi meant. Elani looked thin and pale and ragged, her long black hair without lustre. Peliqua's red braids had faded, and her usually effervescent cream-on-white eyes seemed tired.

"We've been prisoners for a year, Uncle Hochi," Elani said. "I suppose we don't look our best." She smiled wanly.

A year. Gerdi felt his chest tighten. She had been nine winters when he saw her last; she would be ten now. An entire year, a tenth of her life, spent imprisoned. And what about Peliqua? The girl who could never sit still, who always craved activity and action, caged.

"Why. . ." Hochi asked. "Why didn't you just shift? You could hop to Kirin Taq and escape this place."

"I can't, Uncle Hochi," she said. "I can't."

"Why not?"

"I can't *shift* anymore," she replied quietly.

145

Hochi leaned forward, his brow throwing his eyes into darker shadow. "Elani, what happened?" he asked.

So Elani told him, about her attempt to save Kia from the force-bolt that had killed Ty, and how she had been a fraction of a second too late to avoid some of the force of the blast. What had happened to Kia, she did not know; all she knew is that she and Peliqua had rematerialized, in the fields near a village called Shiro; she was unconscious, but Peliqua went to get help from the villagers. They imprisoned her for being a Kirin, and they took Elani as her accomplice. They were held until the local Guardsmen arrived, and then taken to Macaan's palace.

"I can't do it anymore, Uncle Hochi," Elani said. "I tried, but . . . I must have burnt myself out. The shift was all wrong; I messed it up. I think . . . something happened. But I'm not a Resonant anymore, Uncle Hochi. I can't shift now."

"What happened at Macaan's palace?" Gerdi asked.

It was Peliqua that replied. "They knew who El was. They held us there for a long time, saying they'd have a use for us later. I thought they'd forgotten about us after a while, but then . . . just a few cycles – *days* – ago, they moved us. Here. I don't know why."

"But there was something waiting for us when we got here," said Elani, reaching up to her neck and lifting off the pendant she was wearing. "I think it's yours, Uncle Hochi."

For a moment, he just stared. Than he held out his hands, palms upward, as if receiving some holy relic from her. She gave it to him, and he just looked at it, without saying a word, for a long time.

Tochaa's pendant. The eclipsed sun of Kirin Taq, rendered in silver, with an ancient Kirin pictogram in its hollow centre. The thing that he had lost, the symbol of the meaning he had been searching for. Broken Sky.

"How . . . did you. . ." he began, his deep bass voice thin and halting.

"It was on the floor when we were put here," Elani repeated. "S'all I know."

There was silence, as he turned it over in his hand, gazing at it with something close to adoration.

"Y'know, I've had a lot of time to think about it all, while we've been here," said Elani. She reached over and tapped the pendant lightly with her finger. "I think I know what it means."

Hochi leaned back in the darkness, sitting cross-legged in a circle with the others in the cell. "You *know* what Broken Sky means?"

"Then for Cetra's sake, tell him so he can stop ruining his life over it," Gerdi said suddenly, and with a surprising amount of venom.

"What did you say?" Hochi asked, a little hurt.

Gerdi sprang at the opportunity to finally say what had been on his mind for a long time now. "Come on, Hoch. You've been obsessing about that cursed pendant one way or another ever since you got it! It's become some huge thing with you, some kind of redemption. You walk around with this great weight on your shoulders, 'cause you're guilty that you treated Tochaa badly and he ended up saving your life. He's *dead*, Hoch! And you've dedicated every moment since then to solving this imagined puzzle, this stupid task that you think Tochaa set you, because you need something to shift the guilt off your shoulders. Do you know what you've become like over the last few months? I don't even know you anymore!"

There was silence at Gerdi's unusually articulate rant. But for Hochi, the silence brought something else, a memory, that came crashing in on him like a collapsing wall.

*I hit Calica.*

He had hit a woman. The old Hochi would never have done that. The very idea was abhorrent to him. But she had questioned Tochaa's intentions, and he had hit her. And he hadn't even thought about it until now. In fact, it was only since he had seen Elani again, since he had discovered that she was *not* dead that he had begun to feel anything at all outside his cocoon of self-absorption.

*Gerdi's right,* he thought. *Mauni's Eyes, what have I become?*

"Tell me," he said quietly. "Tell me what you think."

"You remember what it means, don't you?" said Elani. "The Koth Macquai gave you the literal translation. *Division, with the eventual hope of unity.* He said it came from an old Kirin folktale. They believed there was once only one world, and that a cataclysm called the Sundering tore it into two: the Dominions and Kirin Taq. You thought that Broken Sky meant unifying the worlds again, and that was what Tochaa wanted you to do. But since Macaan had already *done* that, it didn't make any sense."

Hochi made a small nod. Peliqua shuffled, fidgeting.

"You kinda got it half right, Uncle Hochi. But I don't think Tochaa meant unifying the worlds. Maybe the Sundering never happened, maybe the worlds were always like they are, and some people in the ancient past invented the story. Maybe there were Resonants even back then. I don't know. But I think, if Tochaa meant anything when he gave you that pendant, it wasn't to unify the worlds. It was to unify the *peoples*."

*Don't let Parakka die. Bring it to my people. Show them how to be free.* Tochaa's dying words, from long ago. They came back to Hochi now.

"Look what's been happening, Hoch," said Gerdi, joining in. "Look at what we've done. Most of the Kirins are with us now. The Koth Taraan have come out of hiding and they're on our side. We made peace with the Keriags. I don't even know what else might have gone on while we were busy saving the world. You've been wrapped up with trying to figure out some cryptic dying wish when all the time we were fulfilling it! Macaan's not the enemy, he's just a . . . a. . ."

"Catalyst," Elani provided helpfully. "And when he's gone, when we've all bonded together to defeat him, those bonds will remain. You can't undo what's been done. I've been hearing things from the guards at Macaan's palace, about what's been happening in Kirin Taq. People who have been divided for centuries have found common ground in these last years. That common ground is a hate or fear of Macaan. Y'see, even negative emotions can do some good, Hoch. And a tyrant can be a benefit to us all, even if he doesn't mean to be." She paused, her eyes shining. "You remember I'd been thinking a lot about the two worlds? How everything was connected, balanced? I think I've got it, Uncle Hochi; or most of it, at least. We all have these connections to someone. Calica and Aurin are Splitlings, remember? Aurin's a mixed-blood; she's got Kirin ancestry, and she was born in Kirin Taq. Well everyone's got a Splitling, 'cept Resonants. That means, somewhere in Kirin Taq, there's a Kirin who's *your* Splitling. None of us are so far different as we think. We just need something to make us realize it."

"And that's what Broken Sky is?" Hochi asked slowly, looking at the pendant in his hand.

"It's about *unity*. All races, all people. It's the only way to stop the likes of Macaan keeping us down. It's the only way we can be free."

"No," said a voice from the cell door, and they turned as one at the sound of the lock mechanism opening with a loud clank. "There is a more practical and immediate way of being free."

The door swung open, and in the faint light from outside they saw a tall, thin Machinist, wearing the standard black greatcoat, with a high collar masking his lower face. The top of his head was pale and bald, but a band of metal ran around his skull at eye level, and both his eyes and one ear had been Augmented, along with his left cheek.

There were no guards with him. The only sound was the soft chittering of his goggles, and the whirr of his brass claw-hand.

"My name is Corm," he said, his voice thin and nasal.

Gerdi was already glancing past him, into the dim corridor outside. It was obvious what was crossing all their minds at that moment: *Make a break for it!*

"Oh yes, you can leave whenever you want," he said, catching their looks. "I didn't come here just to make pleasant conversation."

It was too easy. Something was going on. Nobody moved.

"I've heard of you," Gerdi said cautiously. "You're one of Aurin's aides."

"Don't you know? The Princess is dead," Corm replied.

"That's what they say," Gerdi replied. "You know better. She got away from Fane Aracq. You went with her."

It was hard to say how they knew Corm smiled then; his lower face was covered, and his eyes were mechanical goggles. But he did.

"You *are* sharp. Yes, I am the Princess's aide. A special diplomatic attaché. That's why I am outside the rank system that operates within the Guild; it's also why nobody except the Master Machinist can countermand my orders."

"Chiro?" Gerdi asked. "It was *you* who ordered him to keep the cortex key from Macaan?"

"And the one who made contact with Quain. And the one who ordered you to be transferred to this cell. I had to be behind the scenes, of course; it wouldn't do to have Macaan know I am here, when I was supposed to have died with the Princess and Tatterdemalion." He beckoned them out of the cell and, after a moment's hesitation, they got to their feet. "The little girl was transferred here as a hostage. Macaan knows what Ryushi is capable of, and he knows that he will be coming back here with the Parakkan forces in tow. He also knows that Ryushi will not harm Elani, and he hopes to use her as a human shield. I cannot allow that. Now come with me."

"What about Quain?" Gerdi asked.

"Quain has been seen to. Please don't delay."

They got up, looking at each other warily. This

was too good to be true. Another trap? Was it possible?

"Why? Why are you doing all this?" Peliqua asked.

"Because Princess Aurin does not want her father to succeed in his plan. She does not want him to destroy the Dominions."

"*Aurin?*" Gerdi exclaimed in disbelief. "*She's* behind this?"

"Oh yes," Corm replied, fixing him with a dead gaze. "Now do you want to get out of here or don't you?"

"How do you plan to *get* us out?" Hochi asked.

"I have a friend who will help us escape with his own . . . unique method," Corm replied, and he stepped back from the doorway to allow a newcomer into sight. Elani whimpered; Gerdi gathered her behind him.

Framed in the dim light was Tatterdemalion.

# 9

## Anything Fair

Araceil's leathery, bone-armoured wings were spread wide to either side as he soared above the plains and mountains that surrounded the forest bowl where Gar Jenna hid. The sun warmed them from a sky painted with wispy brush strokes of cloud, and clusters of pagoda trees raced by beneath them as they flew. Ryushi lay in the harness on his back, letting Araceil concentrate on keeping them in formation with the rest of the flight while his own mind wandered.

Three days they had been away, four flights of six wyverns and their riders, providing air support for the ground troops and the unstoppable Koth Taraan as they reclaimed the land and towns stolen by Macaan. Now they were heading home, twenty-four of the great creatures, like a flock of enormous birds on their migration. Not a single one of them had fallen on their mission; it had been an unadulterated success.

It had been too easy.

Ryushi was not satisfied. Something was going on. At every battle they had fought, the capitulation of Macaan's troops had been rapid, and in one town they had begun to retreat even before the Parakkans had arrived. It was well known among Parakka that Macaan worked hard to maintain the illusion that his forces were greater and more powerful than they actually were, to prevent the general populace realizing how tenuous his foothold really was; these "soft" battles, clearing his forces from poorly defended towns and minor cities, were never expected to be too challenging for the Parakkan forces.

But their victories were easier than anyone could have guessed. Macaan's troops pulled back at the first sign of assault, heading west towards the Machinists' Citadel; and since their orders were to clear the towns with the minimum of casualties, the Parakkans let them go. They had not forgotten that most of Macaan's Guardsmen were conscripts now, and that there could well be people they once knew beneath those masks.

As the horseshoe shape of low mountains that surrounded the forest of yellow-leaved nanka trees came into view, Ryushi found himself thinking about the Citadel. Parakkan Machinists had said it would take a few days to charge up the boosters that activated the Pulse Hammer. Those few days had probably been used up by now; it would have taken that long to gather all of Parakka's forces in a concerted army. By the time the ground troops that he and the rest of the flight had been supporting arrived – which would be later tonight – then all the pieces should be in place.

The assault on the Machinists' Citadel would start tomorrow. Was tomorrow too late?

His mind flitted over the events that had occurred the last time he had visited the Citadel. He had not had time to deal with them properly since he had returned; he had left almost immediately to join his flight, and the battles that followed had kept him occupied. Now questions and images flew at him. Was Gerdi alright? *Had* Chiro betrayed them, or was there some other explanation? Did Macaan have the cortex key at all?

Strangely, he found himself almost unconcerned about Gerdi's fate. Not that he didn't care; it was just that the Noman boy had such a talent for extricating himself from sticky situations that he found it hard to be worried. Gerdi would be okay, he thought. He always was.

No, it was Hochi and Calica that dwelt largest in his thoughts. The initial heat of his anger at the big man had faded over time, and he began to remember the emotional strain that Hochi was under; after all, he had undergone a gradual change for the worse ever since Tochaa had died in his arms. But that didn't excuse what he did. And it was the *way* that he did it; so cold, as if he were swatting an annoying fly.

*Stop thinking about it. He wanted to be left behind. He wanted to stay with Gerdi. He'll be okay, too.*

He had better be okay, Ryushi thought. I owe him for what he did to Calica.

Calica, then. He had been a little out of control, high on adrenalin and the excitement of having narrowly escaped death, and his body had done what it wanted when he kissed her without any interference from his rational mind. He had already been giddy with ecstasy before he had done it; he hadn't been thinking straight. But after it was done, he didn't regret it. It felt . . . comfortable somehow. It felt *right*.

*It felt like Aurin*, he thought, and instantly shook his head to dispel the unwelcome thought. Aurin was gone. With Calica, it was something different. He had known her for more than two years, and been close friends with her for half that time, before the responsibility of the heartstone and his sister's death separated them. He had become so used to her that he had not even noticed the attraction he felt. After all, she was his first real female friend apart from his sister; he had no benchmark to measure his feelings.

What would he do, now he was returning? He didn't know. He would just go with the flow. It was what he tended to do nowadays.

Araceil screeched happily as the forest bowl came into view, and the flight soared down towards it. Lookouts, invisible in the trees, were already sending signals to retract the great canopy of nanka leaves and branches that concealed Gar Jenna from above.

*Home,* he thought. *Or as close as I'll ever get.*

The wyverns settled on the great metal landing-platform that spanned the river at the bottom of the canyon, having negotiated their way down through the many bridges that linked one side of Gar Jenna to the other. The rushing water roared all around them, sending a wet mist that gently settled into the riders as they disengaged themselves from their harnesses and descended.

"Ryushi!" called a voice as he was sliding off Araceil's flank. It was Calica, running across the platform to him. She looked agitated. "Ryushi, you gotta come. There's trouble."

"I've got to see to Araceil. . ." he began, but she grabbed his arm and pulled him away.

"No time!" she said. "Come on! In the longhouse!"

Ryushi sent a mental apology to Araceil, who patiently folded his four wings and settled himself to wait for someone else to take off his harness. He hurried off the landing platform and into one of the personnel lifts, a wide wicker basket with a door on one side, attached to a winch and pulley overhead. Calica tugged a rope to ring a bell at the top, and the mechanism was activated by the operator. The basket lurched and then began to ascend the side of the canyon.

"What *is* it?" Ryushi asked. Calica was flushed, obviously distressed, and she was breathing hard as if she had run all the way down to meet him.

"It's better if you see. You wouldn't believe me if I told you."

"I'd believe a lot now that I wouldn't have believed two years ago."

"I'm not kidding, Ryushi, you really have to see this one with your own eyes," she said. A few moments later, the lift jerked to a halt and they ran out of it on to one of the lower-level walkways. They followed the aerial streets that clung to the sides of the canyon, passing huts that hugged the rock, their boots clumping on reinforced wooden boards and stamping up stairway after stairway as they went higher and higher. By the time they reached the longhouse – the original longhouse, where Ryushi had once ate when he first came to

Gar Jenna – he was exhausted and Calica was almost dropping.

"In here," she panted, and opened the door. Ryushi peered inside cautiously, but she shoved him in, stepping in after him and closing the door behind her.

He stood there, dumbfounded. It felt as if his insides were melting, that every carefully sectioned and partitioned area of reason or thought within him had suddenly burst its barriers and mixed into one huge, overwhelming and unidentifiable emotion. He could no longer feel the sensations of his skin; he felt disembodied, out of sync with reality in a way that was horribly distressing and incredibly intense.

"Been a while, huh?" said Kia, her face breaking into an uncontrollable grin, tears in her eyes.

"Sis!" Ryushi cried, running across the empty room and hugging her hard.

"Whoa, you got *strong*," she said, hugging him back with equal ferocity.

Calica quietly slipped out of the door, smiling to herself, as the twins spent long minutes simply overcoming the disbelief at the sight of each other again. They exchanged stories, stumbling over their words in an effort to fit them all in as short a time as possible: how Kia had escaped the force-bolt that Jaan had seen obliterate her; how Ryushi had broken free from Aurin's prison in time to seize the heartstone and save the Keriags from extinction; how a year had passed in the desert mines for Kia, and how she had made her way back. They babbled at each other like excited children, until there was a soft knock on the longhouse door and it was opened by Calica.

"Got another little surprise for you," she said, and pushing past her came Elani.

The shock of that on top of the twins' reunion was almost too much for them. Both Kia and Ryushi had thought the little Resonant girl was dead; it had hit Ryushi especially hard, for she represented the last piece of his father, Banto, that he had left. He had promised to protect her with his life before Banto was killed by Takami, and when he heard that Elani had died along with Kia, he thought he had broken that promise. Calica ducked out once more as a fresh round of heartfelt emotion erupted at her appearance.

"I'm sorry, Cousin Kia," Elani said as they embraced. "It was my fault. I couldn't save Ty."

"Ssh, it wasn't your fault," said Kia, and it seemed like she did not have any tears left in her to cry. "You saved *me*. Cetra knows I wished you hadn't at times, but I'm glad now, Elani."

"Hochi and Gerdi are here, too," she said. "They're helping with the preparations at the moment."

"They're alright?" Ryushi exclaimed, forgetting for the moment his quarrel with Hochi. "How?"

"Aurin," said Elani. "Aurin's on our side."

"*Aurin?*" Ryushi and Kia exclaimed in unison, and Elani explained how Corm had been working behind the scenes in the Machinists' Citadel all along, trying to stop Macaan's plan. How he had freed them, and how Tatterdemalion had taken them through a mirror to the outside.

"But weren't the Jachyra mostly responsible for taking over the Citadel in the first place?" Ryushi asked.

"They can't disobey the King's orders," said Elani. "They've got those stones inside them, like the Keriag Queens had. Macaan can kill them just like *that*," she snapped her fingers. "But they can go behind his back. They *hate* him, Cousin Ryushi. They hate him for making them like they are. It's Aurin they're loyal to, not him. And Aurin doesn't want him to destroy the Dominions. 'Cause that's what he's going to do, he's gonna—"

"I know, El," said Ryushi, laying a comforting hand on her shoulder. "I know. We're gonna stop him."

"You better," said Elani. "It wouldn't be fair if we lost now."

"Since when was anything fair?" Kia said gravely, and their high spirits were dampened a little; but only for a moment, for nothing could keep down the joy they felt at seeing each other again, the three who had begun their journey together from Osaka Stud many seasons ago, and as they talked and laughed, they knew that they would end it together as well.

One way or another.

Araceil never got a chance to have his harness removed. After the initial warmth of their reunion, Kia said that she had some people she wanted

Ryushi to meet. He had thought he would be drained after his journey and from the excitement of seeing his sister and cousin, but the reality was just the opposite. So he promised to come back and see Elani later on, and they made their way to where Araceil waited. Kia had told him that they were camped a way off, for Gar Jenna's location was still a secret and both Jedda and Li'ain had insisted on staying with the desert-folk.

Ryushi thought about Calica on their journey down. He felt vaguely guilty about not having a chance to talk to her, but his feet had hardly touched the ground since he returned from his mission.

Araceil, of course, knew at the moment Ryushi did that he would be flying again. Ryushi's question to him, asking him without words if he was too tired and did he mind going on another trip, was answered before Kia had finished her request that he come and meet Jedda and Li'ain. The thought processes that the two shared were so close that it was like asking himself a question. He already knew that Araceil was not particularly worn out, and that he was happy to take them, sharing as he did in Ryushi's elation at seeing his sister again. They had to adjust the harness to add another seat, but they were soon on their way, back out over the sunny plains towards the camp of the desert-folk.

From high up, the extent of the Parakkan forces became apparent at last. There were several encampments in view, a few dozen miles from each other; there were many more out of sight, hidden by the flat line of the horizon. They were spread out all over the plains that made up most of the central part of the Dominions; clusters of tents, of all different colours. There, the forces that had been mustered from the mountains; over there, the militia of the western villages; and there, like a slowly shuffling herd of boulders, an army of Koth Taraan heading northward. Tomorrow, they would disperse to their tasks; some to assault the Machinists' Citadel, where almost all of Macaan's forces were massed, and some to defend the cities and towns against the onslaught that was to come.

The creatures from Deepwater. Was it possible?

They headed southwards, to where the multi-coloured tents of the desert-folk were clustered. It was necessary to have the forces as far apart as possible, so as not to draw attention to the location of Gar Jenna, which sat on the northwestern edge of the plains, at the foot of the mountains. If the attack on Macaan was not successful, Gar Jenna might still profit by remaining secret. By having them assemble on the central plains, they had chosen neutral territory, and the different forces had more than enough space to avoid getting in each other's way.

"We're doing it," said Kia, over the rush of the wind. "We're really doing it! Could you imagine, two winters ago, that we'd have the best of *two worlds* coming together to fight Macaan?"

Ryushi grinned over his shoulder. "Not bad for a couple of ignorant mountain kids, huh?"

"Yeah, like it was all *our* doing," Kia chided, batting him on the arm. "Don't hog the credit."

Araceil glided down into a shallow dive, and Ryushi brought him in to settle on the edge of the nomad encampment. All the tribes were here, together, under the banner of an uneasy truce. Kia's pacification of the Sa'arin and their subsequent defeat of Takami had given them cause to believe that they could operate as an effective alliance, but there were still old blood feuds simmering that would not be placated so easily.

The wyvern touched down smoothly, absorbing the shock of the landing with the huge muscles of his legs; two people were already on their way out to meet the newcomers as they unstrapped their harnesses and got down from Araceil's back.

"This is them," said Kia, hurrying Ryushi over to meet the tall, dark-skinned Rai'kel and the newly recovered Li'ain. Kia still had to confront Li'ain over the events of the battle, but she told herself that now was not the time. In the end, it didn't matter; if she had known how soon her questions would be answered, she would not have worried.

"Ryushi," she said. "This is Jedda and Li'ain."

But Ryushi's face was a picture of surprise; he hadn't thought that the day had anything left in store for him, but he was proved wrong now.

"Ryushi," said Li'ain, offering him a tentative smile.

*Aurin*, he thought, but he didn't say a word.

# 10

## Something Between Them

Night fell over Gar Jenna, but the sounds of preparation never stopped. Pulleys whined as they hauled heavy loads, footsteps ran back and forth, wyverns winged overhead, running messages between the camps on the plains. But in the cool of the nanka forest, where the bright moonglow filtered through the thin leaves of the trees and turned their yellow to blue-white, the sounds were only distant, a faint percussion to the noises of the forest-creatures that pipped and crackled and chattered in the shadows.

Ryushi walked through the trees with Aurin – she who had been Li'ain all this time – and as the pale light slid over her he saw how much she had changed since he had last known her. The hair was the most obvious; she wore it down now, in a long cascade over her shoulders. She wore little make-up, and her clothes were not the elegant gown of court but sturdy, practical travel clothes. She walked differently, less of the Princess about her and her speech had been coloured by other dialects. She had lost her habit of finishing her sentences imperiously with "yes?", and her pale skin was tanned. She looked like a traveller now. Who would guess she had once been royalty?

"So tell me what happened, Aurin," Ryushi said. He was still a little wary around her. They might have had something between them once, an impossible relationship between a prisoner and his captor; but they had also been mortal enemies in their time, and it was not easily forgotten.

"It is Li'ain, now," she said. "Aurin is a name I will never bear again."

"Li'ain, then. It's been a year?"

"A year," she agreed.

"Where have you been?"

She was silent for a time, thinking. The faint scent of desert-flowers drifted around her. "Searching," she said after a time.

"For me?"

She smiled wanly. "I knew where you were all the time. How do you think I knew where Gar Jenna was?

"Tatterdemalion," Ryushi said.

"*All* the Jachyra," she replied. "They found you, in the end, while you were in Kirin Taq. They found Gar Jenna, too, a season ago. Parakka has become so big, with so many boughs and branches, it is impossible to hide from spies like the Jachyra now. It only takes one careless slip for them to follow the branch to the trunk."

"You've *known*? For months?"

"Oh yes," she said. "But do not worry. My father is as ignorant as he ever was. It is not in my interests to see him win. And the Jachyra are *mine*."

For a moment, he saw a flash of the old Princess there, the pride and the haughtiness of a young ruler. It stirred something inside him, reminding him of how he had once felt for her, allowing him to taste the flavour before receding again.

"So what were you searching for?" he said.

"A way to make it up to you. To everyone," she replied, gazing ahead down the shadowy path they walked. "But mostly to you."

"You found Kia. You brought her back," Ryushi said, running his fingertips along the smooth trunks of the trees they passed.

"Is it enough?" Aurin asked.

"More than enough," he replied, thinking how he had betrayed her in Fane Aracq.

Silence again, as Li'ain searched for the words to say.

"I was . . . I have learned a lot this last year. You remember you told me once, that what I was doing . . . executing whole villages, sending families to the mines . . . you said to me that it was because I did not know any better. I hated you then, for patronizing me. But I think you were right." She paused, emotion threatening her voice. "I know better now. I have lived among the people I would once have killed. I have been befriended by some and rejected by just as many. I have been used and mistreated, and I have used and mistreated others; but I have also been shown more kindness than any stranger deserves, and I have seen self-sacrifice that would put the noblest warrior to shame." She looked up at him, meeting his eyes at last. "When you took the heartstone, you threw me into your world, Ryushi. It is an ugly and cruel place. But it is also more beautiful than I could have imagined. And I am ashamed at the ignorance of the woman who, only a year ago, was the ruler of an entire land." She laughed mirthlessly. "I did not even *want* it. Can you imagine how spoiled, how ungrateful that sounds? I had the lives of every Kirin in my hand, every ship and city, and I did not care for it. I thought only about what it meant to *me* to be the Princess, and not once about what it meant to *them*."

"Stop beating yourself up about it, Aurin. Guilt won't do you any good," Ryushi said, thinking of Hochi.

"Oh, but it *does*," she said. "It was my fault that Takami attacked Base Usido. It was my fault that he nearly killed Kia. And it was guilt that made me find her again. Because I knew I could never come back, not without some kind of atonement."

"Why come back at all?" asked Ryushi. "Why take the risk? You know if anyone else recognizes you, you'll probably be killed."

"Who is there who knows me?" Li'ain asked. "Nobody in Parakka has seen my face, or few enough not to matter. Your own sister did not know me."

"Count your blessings with that one," Ryushi replied.

"Thank you, Ryushi," she said slowly. "For not revealing me."

"It'd be the same as having you executed. I didn't let you go in Fane Aracq so I could get you killed now." He stopped walking. "But I didn't let you go so you could come *back*, either."

The hurt was plain on Li'ain's face, and once again she felt the frustration that she had experienced when they had first met, that a single person had the power to wound her so deeply or give her such happiness with a word. "You did not want me to come back?"

"Aurin—" he began.

"Li'ain," she corrected him, but he held up a hand.

"No. It's Aurin. You can change your name, but it doesn't change anything else. Remember who you *are*! You can make it up to me, but you can't make it up to *everyone*. How can you come to Gar Jenna? How can you just walk into the home of your enemies and hope than none of them recognizes you? What if I'd decided to tell everyone?"

"I knew you wouldn't."

"But what if I *had*?"

"I came back here for you," she said. The pronouncement hung in the moonlight between them. They stood, surrounded by the trees and the sounds of the night, and faced each other.

Then Ryushi averted his eyes. "It's not like it was, Aurin."

"Is there another?" she asked, each word like a crystal of ice.

"No. Maybe," he replied. "It's not the point."

"What is?"

He looked at his hands, as if he held inspiration in his palms, and shook his head. "What did you expect, Aurin? You knew it couldn't work, even in Fane Aracq. You and me.

177

You think it can work now? Every day lived under the threat of you being discovered? I'm still not even sure you're not secretly working for Macaan."

"Oh, you are being ridiculous," she snapped, and at once she was the girl he had known, the colour high in her cheeks, her eyes flashing. "If I'd wanted to, I could have betrayed you a thousand times over. If I wanted to, I could destroy Gar Jenna as I destroyed Takami's camp, and that would put an end to your precious resistance!" She stepped closer to him, challenging. "*If* I wanted to."

"But you don't," he said.

"No!" she said, stalking in agitated circles. "Because of *you*, I have come to love this land that my father wants to destroy. Oh, make no mistake, he *is* going to destroy it. His mind is on suicide now that he knows he has lost. The Jachyra know that much. But I will not allow him to take the Dominions with him. He will die, and I will be free." She fixed him with a steady gaze. "But what of *you*, Ryushi? What will *you* do when this is all over? Because I will not wait for your

178

pleasure, for you to decide if I am worthy of you or not. Choose, and choose soon, or one day I will not be here."

And with that, she turned and was gone, disappearing into the forest, leaving Ryushi alone.

"Hi, Kia," Calica said, without turning around from where she leaned on the walkway guardrail, looking down at the faint slashes of moonlight that shivered along the surface of the river that ran beneath Gar Jenna.

"Calica," Kia said warily. She had just come back from seeing Hochi and Gerdi, and had been walking back to a hut that had been designated her quarters until tomorrow, avoiding the areas where there was most traffic. The bustle of preparation had made some walkways heavily congested; everyone had cause to be thankful tonight for the skilful construction of the supports and guardrails that kept them safe.

"Sorry to meet you like this; I knew you'd be coming down this way."

"Your stones, huh?"

"Yeah."

Kia walked over to her, leaning on her elbows and back against the rail. The dark abyss beneath, pierced with a thousand orange glowstones, did not bother her in the least. The rails were as sturdy as it was possible to be.

"What's on your mind?" she said.

"Us," Calica said. She sighed, and then straightened and looked at Kia, brushing the orange-gold cascade of her hair back from her face. "Us. You and me have always been at odds, haven't we?"

"Pretty much," Kia said.

"It's. . ." she began, stopped, and started again. "I was glad when you came back, Kia. We all thought you were gone." She paused. "I think we should make an effort. For Ryushi's sake. To get along."

Kia smiled. "I'd been thinking about that," she said, tilting her head back and looking up at the levels and walkways that leaned over them. "You don't have anything to be sorry for. I know why I was like I was. I think . . . all along I realized you were Aurin's Splitling, y'know? Subconsciously. And you know how much I just love Macaan's family." She rounded the last sentence off with a sarcastic wink.

"Don't we all?" Calica replied.

"That wasn't the whole thing, though," Kia continued. "I guess . . . y'know, I was jealous. Of how Ryushi was with you. I *am* his twin, after all. No one likes to lose their other half. I think . . . I just replaced him with Ty. But I still wanted him around. You were a threat to all that, I suppose." She shrugged. "Whatever. I'm sorry, Calica. You wanna wipe the slate clean? Start again?"

Calica wore a vague expression of surprise. "Sure," she said. "You mean it?"

"Course I do," Kia said, extending a hand. Calica took it. "People have died, worlds have been won and lost, history is being written right now. I think us two bitching at each other seems kinda petty in comparison, don't you think?"

Calica laughed. "I'm happy you feel that way."

"And I won't tell Ryushi. About what happened with you and our mother."

Calica felt a chill at her words, but she managed to smile gratefully. "I appreciate that."

"You know you'll have to tell him sometime, though."

"I know."

They shared the quiet for a time, looking out into the darkness, before Kia spoke again.

"In the spirit of our newfound alliance, I'd better offer you a sisterly warning," she said. She made a motion with her hand towards the trees at the top of the canyon. "That Li'ain girl. Watch out for her."

"What do you mean?" Calica asked.

"I know what you and Ryushi have got between you. Elani saw it seasons ago. I didn't want to believe it then, but . . . well, it's pretty obvious now. And you're blushing, by the way. Anyhow, as to Li'ain. If you wanna keep my brother, don't leave those two alone too long."

Calica gave a derisive snort. "He's not going to elope with someone he's just met, even if we *didn't* have anything between us. And we don't," she added. What had happened beneath the Machinists' Citadel was a secret still; a kiss, even several, might mean the world or nothing at all. She was practical enough to wait until she had a chance to talk to Ryushi before shooting her mouth off. But oh, the child inside her *wanted* to. . .

"It's Aurin, Calica. It's the ex-Princess Aurin that's with him out in the forest."

A moment of shock passed over Calica's face, then she frowned, not really believing. "It can't be."

"We know the rumours about what happened between them while Ryushi was a prisoner in Fane Aracq. We know she escaped, even if everyone else thinks she died. She's been lying to me ever since I met her, and I always wondered why. I knew she was hiding something. I had my suspicions when I saw her waste Takami's encampment. I mean, she's got power that puts Ryushi's to shame. Eight spirit-stones, by my reckoning. *Eight*. You'd have to be *very* rich to invest that much in one child."

"That doesn't prove anything," said Calica, sounding a little churlish as she tried to deny it. A slight panic was beginning to swell behind her words. "None of that means—"

"You didn't see Ryushi's face when he met

her," Kia interrupted. "I may not have seen him for a while, but I can still read my own twin. He *knew* her. And that clinched it for me. All the other stuff made sense then. You know about my time in the mines? It was Tatterdemalion who found me through my mirror, who was putting all that stuff in my room, sneaking in at night. Y'know, I think when I stole that reflector, I knew what I was doing, without realizing it. I think I'd rather have been killed by the Jachyra than stay in those mines. At least then, I'd remember before I died. Go out on my feet." She paused, looking into the distance. "They were trying to jog my memory, without allowing themselves to be seen. Trying to make me remember enough to want to break out. They couldn't just carry me through the mirror; if I saw a Jachyra, I'd know who was behind it. This whole thing, my rescue, everything . . . it's all just been part of Aurin's plan to get back to Ryushi."

Calica couldn't think of anything to say through the shock of Kia's words, so she spoke the first thought that crossed her mind. "That's some effort she's made."

"Uh-huh. And she may not give up easily."

"Hang on," said Calica, shaking her head and turning suddenly angry. "What in *Cetra* are we doing arguing about this? If that's Aurin down there, let's go get her! What about you; don't *you* owe her for what's happened to your family?"

"It's Ryushi's call," said Kia. "We've gotta trust him. If he doesn't want to reveal her, we have to respect that."

"Why? Because he's too love-struck to recognize a viper when he sees one?" Calica cried.

"That's jealousy talking," Kia said bluntly. "Aurin may be one of the most dangerous people alive, but she also saved my life, and she helped the desert-folk win a great victory. Corm and Tatterdemalion, on her orders, have been working secretly to further her interests – which at the moment happen to coincide with ours – and between the three of them they've done more than Parakka ever could." She rubbed the nape of her neck, as if remembering the red ponytail that used to hang there. "I know she could just be setting us up. She's got Whist on her side for one thing, and we know just how trustworthy *he* is. But right at the moment she's one of the most potent allies we've got. Because with her come the Jachyra." Kia shrugged. "We can't interfere without blowing the whole thing. We've gotta let Ryushi handle this."

Calica slapped the guardrail with her palm in frustration. "Just *once* I'd like things to be straightforward," she snapped. Then, seeing Kia's amused smile, she softened. "You heard about the plans?"

"Vaguely," Kia replied. "Fill me in."

"Okay. Sections of the army are travelling to the coastal towns and cities to do what they can about defending them against the Deepwater monsters."

"*If* the Pulse Hammer works," said Kia. "It's still a prototype, remember?"

"I think we can rely on the fact that it will," said Calica. "When have we ever lucked out *that* much?"

Kia made a face that said: *Guess so.*

"Anyway, the main bulk of the force is going for the assault on the Machinist's Citadel. What we intend to do is take in a small strike force, get them inside the Citadel and destroy the Pulse Hammer while everyone is occupied outside."

"How?"

"Same way as before. I mean, not that particular entrance, but there are other ways. We still have Corm on the inside."

"You'd never get all the way through to the Pulse Hammer with the Citadel on full alert," said Kia. "They'll be guarding it with everything they've got."

Calica shrugged. "We can only try."

"I've got a better idea," said Kia. "But it's gonna take the co-operation of Ryushi's new friend. So behave yourself, Calica. We still need her."

Calica scowled, and thought of Ryushi alone in the forest with her Splitling, and burned inside.

At dawn the next day, the lookouts in the trees above Gar Jenna observed what appeared to be a massive ripple in the sky, stretching from horizon to horizon, that blew the clouds into tatters before it as it raked eastward. The phenomenon lasted for only a second, so fast was it travelling. Several moments later, the sky boomed as if with thunder, and the earth shivered. Then all was peace again.

The lookouts signalled to each other, their faces grim. It had been the birthing-cry of the Pulse Hammer, operational at last.

The final battle had begun.

*How will it end?*

*You'll have to read*

# Broken Sky

## Part Nine

*and find out. . .*